Otto

and the Flying Twins

Charlotte Haptie had a number of sensible jobs before writing *Otto and the Flying Twins*. It is her first book. She was brought up in Buckinghamshire and Merseyside and now lives in Scotland. She thinks that writing, like any sort of invention, is unpredictable and mysterious. Perhaps you would like to write a book yourself. If so, don't be put off. Just start.

Otto
and the Flying Twins

A TALE OF THE *Karmidee*

Charlotte Haptie

Hodder
Children's
Books

a division of Hodder Headline Limited

This book was written
with the loyal support of my family and friends.
It is dedicated to them with affection.

Contents

THE City OF Trees

CrabFace

TumbleMan

The Rainmaker

7

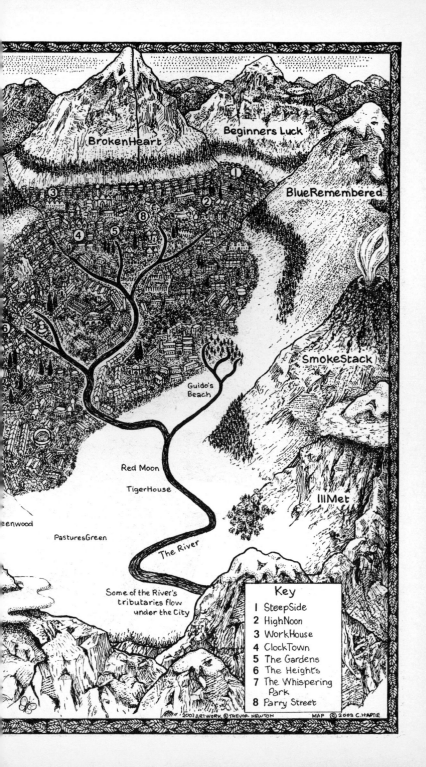

BrokenHeart

Beginners Luck

BlueRemembered

① SteepSide

② HighNoon

③ WorkHouse

④ ClockTown

⑤ The Gardens

⑥

⑦

⑧ Parry Street

SmokeStack

Guido's Beach

IllMet

Red Moon

TigerHouse

eenwood

PasturesGreen

The River

Some of the River's
tributaries flow
under the City

Key

1 SteepSide
2 HighNoon
3 WorkHouse
4 ClockTown
5 The Gardens
6 The Heights
7 The Whispering
   Park
8 Parry Street

2002 ARTWORK © TREVOR NEWTON   MAP © 2002 C. HAPTIE

HOW THE  CITY BEGAN

Once upon a time the world was full of magic. Mermaids in the sea, dragons dreaming on the edge of volcanoes, little people, giants, sorcerers . . . But the human beings are relentless. They have trampled everywhere and anything strange or magical has been forced to hide. Who wants to be put in an aquarium or a zoo, or worse, a laboratory? Who wants to be stared at, poked at, always different, maybe even mistrusted and feared and accused of terrible things?

That is how the Karmidee, the magical people of all races, came to build their secret City of Trees. Far away, ringed by savage mountains, it was safe for hundreds of years. Until an earthquake cracked one mountain through the heart and the humans found the way inside.

1

Explorers, outsiders, normal people. Relentless.

They found something new and beautiful and extraordinary and they wanted it all for themselves.

The Karmidee ended up living on the mud flats and the river, where they were left alone.

Then something mysterious happened and the City closed in on itself once more. As the centuries passed the outsiders who had settled there came to believe it had always been theirs. They couldn't remember very much about the rest of the world and they thought many things respectable and normal which were actually impossible and magical.

Meanwhile the widges, the artists, the lamp-eyes, the mat-flyers, the few multiples, the rare and elusive dammerung and all the other Karmidee waited for the next chapter in their story to begin.

THE FireBox LAUNDERETTE

It was evening in the great and mysterious City of Trees. The summer sky was violet and the streets rattled with the sound of trams taking people home.

Otto Hush and his father Albert walked to the FireBox Launderette. Albert carried the big bag of washing. Otto had the packet of soap flakes.

The FireBox was large, ornate and brightly lit by chandeliers full of candles. Tea, coffee and raspberry juice were available from the wind-up drinks machine. The washing machines gleamed. They were driven by steam. The whole room was alive with a thunderous chugging. Conversation was impossible.

Otto perched on a table and gazed contentedly out of the

windows. 'FireBox Launderette', it said across the glass in an arc of spiky letters, mirror-writing from Otto's perspective – 'Wash your cares away. Today and every day'.

Albert unfolded his newspaper. It was a routine of theirs coming to the FireBox on a Friday.

The driers were Otto's favourite part. They were in a separate room, with carved wooden panels round the walls. They spun slowly and quietly and if you opened the door you could feel the rhythmic blasts of hot air. Your clothes came out smelling of liquorice.

This evening, however, all was not going well in the drying room. People were complaining and putting damp clothes into their bags. The driers weren't hot.

'That's weird, isn't it, Dad,' said Otto. 'They've never gone wrong before.'

The machines stopped altogether and a voice crackled anxiously out of a speaker on the wall.

'Very sorry. Problem with the drying facilities. Not working due to illness. Free fairy cakes. Please collect your refund at the desk. The Launderette will now close.'

'That's weird, isn't it, Dad,' said Otto. 'Who's ill do you think? Machines don't get ill, do they?'

Albert, a quiet man, raised his eyebrows. He had started filling the drier with wet clothes. Now, unhurriedly, he began to take them out again.

Just then a door opened in the panelled wall and a tall woman came through it looking worried and carrying a tin. Presumably the fairy cakes.

'Very sorry,' she repeated sternly to everyone as she pushed the tin underneath their noses, 'very sorry. Most unusual.'

She almost fell over Otto who was looking for a lost sock on the floor. Then she turned and came nose to nose with Albert.

Otto saw them acknowledge one another with a quick nod of the head.

'Mr Albert Hush,' said the woman in a low voice.

'Madame Morgan le Grey,' said Albert. 'My son Otto,' he added.

She gave Otto an extremely sharp look.

The last customers tramped past them to the door.

An unexpected coughing sound came from the driers and small clouds of ash billowed out through several of the open doors.

'Mr Hush,' said Morgan le Grey, 'how remarkable that you should be here today.' She glanced again at Otto. 'We have a problem with our, with our machinery and we can't get hold of the, of the mechanic on the, er, phone and—'

'I understand,' interrupted Albert. 'You know, in my work in the library I don't get much opportunity to use all my skills, I may be a little out of practice . . .'

'But I fear it may soon become a matter of life and death, and he trusts you, you've helped him in the past and he remembers that, Mr . . . Hush.'

Otto noticed that she paused a tiny scary moment before she said the name, and she stared at his father very hard.

Then Albert told Otto to wait and he and Morgan le Grey went through the door in the wall.

Otto sat alone in the drying room. It was all so strange. Who was this person who trusted Albert and what could that have to do with the driers not working?

More spluttering sounds from the driers.

Then he noticed that the sock he'd been searching for was stuck at the back of the one they'd been going to use.

He was small and the drier was big. If anyone had come into the room at that moment they would have seen only his feet sticking out.

He had the sock and was about to wriggle backwards when there was a very loud cough and then a groaning and gasping. All of this came through the vent at the back of the drier. This must be where the hot air came in, of course.

It was like listening down a tube.

Then, quite distinctly, he heard his father's voice,

'. . . this bit of coal . . . stuck in the left flame gland . . .

should be all right now with a few days' rest and the mixture . . . I've written it down here.'

There was a thumping sound.

'. . . standing up already . . . good sign,' continued Albert inexplicably, wherever he was.

And then Morgan le Grey, '. . . very frisky nature . . . only young . . .'

Then a massive scratching and scuffling, like giant claws on the floor, and Otto heard his father give a yell of pain.

'Let go you stupid creature!' shouted Morgan le Grey.

'Calm yourself, calm yourself,' came Albert's voice, '. . . just trying to get his jaws open.'

Otto scrambled out of the drier, ran to the panelled door, flung it open and found himself in a short dark passage which led to a second door.

'Put him down at once, FB!'

Otto opened the second door and stopped short.

Morgan le Grey had her back to him and was jumping about with her arms outstretched.

Something that looked a bit like a dinosaur was rearing up in front of them and banging its head on the ceiling. It was purple, Otto noticed, although this was hardly the point. The point was that it was holding Albert in its mouth by his leg.

'Calm, calm,' Albert kept saying as he swung through the air.

'Put him down!' yelled Morgan le Grey, waving what looked like an extra large stick of liquorice.

The creature did put Albert down then. Otto thought it had seen him in the doorway and he darted back behind the door. He was so shocked that afterwards he didn't remember getting back to the drying room.

It didn't seem long before Albert and Morgan le Grey returned. Albert with a tear in his trousers just below the knee.

'Thank you so much,' Morgan le Grey kept repeating in her stern voice. 'If there's ever any way we can return the favour . . .'

'We may both come to a day,' said Albert gravely, 'when we recall those honourable words.'

They took the tram home to Parry Street. As usual they got off at the stop next to the Tourist Information Office where the friendly woman behind the desk never seemed to have much to do.

In through the doors of Hershell Buildings, past the concierge, Mrs Thudbutton, scowling behind her newspaper.

Clank, clank from the lift gates. The lift, like everything else about the building, was elegant and old.

Up the stairwell to the fifth floor. Smells of cooking. Sound of someone's radio as they passed a front door. Worn red carpets and creaky floorboards.

Albert humming to himself as he turned the key in the lock.

Then the twins came stumping and staggering towards them and Dolores followed wiping her hands on her apron.

Albert kissed her on the cheek.

'What's happened to the washing, it's all wet,' she said a moment later.

Otto looked expectantly from one parent to the other but all Albert said was, 'Problem with the driers.'

Then he picked up the twins and took them off for their bath.

MAYOR Crumb

Later on, just before Otto had his bath, Mayor Crumb came on the television. You couldn't escape him unless you turned it off because there was only one channel.

Albert was all for giving him the button. Dolores wanted to leave it on. In the end they all saw it.

'Fellow citizens,' said Mayor Crumb, bun-faced and sticky as ever, 'I wanted to have one of our chats. Recently there have been some strange incidents in the city. Deep holes have been appearing in the roads. Sometimes the trams cannot run. Many of you must know about it. At first I hoped that these were natural events, small earthquakes perhaps. Citizens, if only I could say that was true. Alas. Investigations have shown that it may have been caused by magicos. Whether they intend it or not they are enemies of the City. Enemies right here in our midst.'

He paused for a moment.

'You won't have heard of Councillor Elfina Crink, she only joined the council recently and doesn't appear in public because of her heavy workload and her extreme dedication to her work. This morning I appointed her Minister for Modernization and she would like to address you. Councillor Crink.'

The camera swerved to the left and revealed a pale woman sitting next to the Mayor.

Albert breathed in sharply.

'Greetings, citizens,' said Elfina Crink. She spoke almost without moving her face at all. 'Don't let this crisis worry you. There are people hanging round the streets, sitting in the parks, sitting on the beach, doing weird tricks for money, begging and drinking bloodberry juice and looking scruffy and magical. You all know who I mean. We are certain that some of them were responsible for these outrageous holes in the road. They are much more dangerous than they appear. They have magical powers which they can't control. As you know parts of the moonstone mines have recently had to close because of rock falls. No doubt this is something to do with the magicos also.'

'I don't believe this,' whispered Albert.

'Ssh!' said Dolores.

The Mayor appeared on the screen again.

'From now on we are going to be just like the Outside,' he said proudly. 'I'm setting up a new police force, the Normal Police. I'm depending on you to give them all the help you can. They will remove anything that is not Normal, respectable, possible and modern. From now on all magicos will be found useful employment. Let us rise for the new City Anthem.'

He stood up himself, and his head disappeared briefly off the top of the screen before the camera could catch up with him.

Very loud music suddenly started and Albert turned the television off.

There was a silence in the Hush family living room.

'I don't believe this,' said Albert at last. 'This is horrible.'

'Well there are a lot of them about, Al, just hanging around. And everyone knows they've got these powers. And no one is ever sure what the powers are. I mean maybe they could flatten the place overnight. I don't know. And they all live down there in the mud towns in those funny looking houses and boats and things. Some of them look very creepy.'

But Albert seemed not even to hear his wife properly. He seemed to be talking to himself.

'I don't believe this,' he whispered again. 'It can't be true.'

Otto was on the floor building a tower of bricks for Hepzibah. He looked up and saw his father's face.

'What's the matter, Dad?'

'And anyway,' said Dolores peacefully, 'why would the Mayor lie to us?'

Why indeed?

That night Albert Hush lay awake.

He was a rare and deep-thinking man and, unlike other citizens, he had taken the trouble to study anything he could find about the Karmidee.

There was a tangled puzzle of stories and drawings in the Ancient Documents Archive of the Central Library on the Boulevard. Albert was a Senior Librarian and he had created the Archive himself. It contained hundreds of documents and he had examined each of them. He even knew where some of them had been found and when and how. Sometimes packages would arrive, even now, usually by night, with papers or pictures inside and a letter, unsigned, addressed simply to The Library.

Karmidee didn't visit the library much. But long ago, of course, they had built it.

Albert gave up trying to sleep and paced around the flat.

He was angry and afraid and tormented by half-formed and horrible forebodings. All night he scoured his mind, the

encyclopedia of his knowledge. Trying to understand what was happening.

Trying to find the beginning.

THE Raft

The beginning had been many years before.

Someone was searching.

Perhaps every story starts that way.

The two children had built the raft together out of logs and barrels. After three summers it was the best they had ever made. Quietly they punted through the green water under the stilt houses.

A steamy mist surrounded them. Boats, walkways, jetties and houses were hidden. Then suddenly looming. Then lost again.

'It's a long way,' said the girl. 'We'll have to go faster than this.'

'It probably won't still be there,' said the boy.

'It will, it will, no one will have noticed. And there's money in it, I bet, or jewels or . . . watch out!'

Something like a grey rope curled out of the water just in front of them.

'Mud snake,' said the boy calmly.

The tail flicked and was gone.

'I thought it was one of those swamp dragons,' she said.

'They're very, very rare and they're five times the size.'

'Well you should know . . . Now! Look over there, further down.'

'I'm not going much further,' said the boy in his quiet voice. 'I'm going to be late home as it is.'

'There!' she cried.

A ragged tree stood alone on the bank. The water had washed the ground away from between its roots, probably in the last flood, and the girl had seen it when she came past on her father's boat the day before.

A box was stuck there, still half buried.

'You didn't say it was under a tree.'

'So what? If it's money I want three-quarters because I saw it first.' She was already mooring the raft to the roots.

He smiled to himself because she was always like this, and now she was tugging at the box and fighting with it as if it was alive.

The Raft

'Careful,' he said.

It suddenly came free. She fell backwards and it flew from her hands and bounced on the ground. The lid broke from its rusty hinges and something fell out.

It was a package wrapped in oilskin and it didn't look like money.

The boy bent to pick it up but she pushed him out of the way and ripped at the strips of leather that held it fast. They were crisp with age and one snapped between her fists.

It wasn't money. It was a roll of parchment.

She was almost crying with frustration.

'Just some stupid picture!'

'Here, let me—'

She held it out of his reach. 'There's some weird writing, I can't even read it, some primitive magico stuff.'

She kicked the box into the water.

He scowled. She used to bite her tongue on those sorts of words when she was with him. Recently she'd been using them more and more.

'I think I know what it is and we mustn't look at it,' he said. 'We must give it back to the tree.'

'Give it back to the tree. What are you bleating about?'

'It's Karmidee.'

'Yeah, well, I guessed that. Look, there's a woman,

standing on a pile of money. She's holding something like little houses. The City. The Town Hall's there, see. She's holding the City except it's small, like a doll's house. And she's got numbers on her clothes. And here's a bit of writing, what does it say?'

He sighed. 'It's the old language of the Karmidee. Let's put it back. We shouldn't look.'

'It might be worth something.'

'Karmidee stuff isn't worth anything. Not to Normals, citizens. And they're the only ones with any money. We must put it back.'

But she wouldn't give up. 'Read me something. Read me something and I'll give it to you and you can put it back then.'

He stared at the writing which looked very old.

She was watching him. 'It's weird, isn't it? I'm the one who's a citizen and yet you're the one who can do things, like read different languages, even though you're just—'

'Here's a bit,' said the boy, 'hang on, a warrior, no, warrior-like, a woman, a sort of leader becomes the richest citizen who has ever lived, had ever lived. Or would have ever lived.'

'Well has it happened or not?'

'Not necessarily. What this person who wrote this wanted

to say was about a possible future. Probably more than one possible future. That's why we shouldn't read it.'

'You mean it's not real?'

He was thinking of a way to explain. 'The person is sort of dreaming something. Maybe it's happened by now, maybe not yet. Maybe it never will.'

'Anyway there's a woman standing on a pile of money. Then there's some writing. Get on with it.'

'OK, I'm finding where I was, here we are . . .

> "How can she be stopped? How can the beloved
> city be saved? What will happen if we deny
> ourselves, if we forget the beginning? If the enemy
> we despise is really in our hearts?" '

'Sounds like a load of rubbish to me,' she said scornfully.

He continued, ignoring her, 'Then there are these pictures and it says here . . .

> "The two that were one become one again."

. . . or something like that,' he frowned, 'I can't really say any more. It's like a puzzle. These numbers on her dress, here, 6 and 8 and 48, they probably mean something. We shouldn't have looked. These things are dangerous.'

'No wonder you people all live down here and don't have proper jobs, you've got your heads in cloud-cuckoo land.'

Darkness was coming through the mist and it was getting hard to see. Suddenly the water seemed to come alive. It began to surge and suck all around the raft. Waves were coming from nowhere, getting bigger, washing right up to where they were standing.

They both jumped and the girl dropped the parchment. He got to it first and jammed it down the front of his shirt.

'Swamp dragon!' he shouted.

They scrambled higher up the bank and the river seemed to burst out of itself, pulling the tree up out of the mud and smashing it away. Other boxes, buried deeper, came up with the last of the roots and were gone. Below they saw their raft leap right out of the water and then plunge down in a churning broth of bubbles and slime.

The boy caught a glimpse of a great scaled head, studded with barnacles, two clever eyes and a ruff of gills. The creature gave a terrible roar and then dived out of sight. A whirlpool spun in its wake.

Everything was still again.

The broken pieces of the raft came to the surface and floated slowly downstream.

For a moment they couldn't speak.

'Good thing we weren't on it,' she said eventually.

Still they didn't move, both shaking, although it wasn't cold.

The Raft

'Well you can't give it back to the tree now, or whatever you said, because there isn't a tree to give it back to any more.'

Without saying much more they set off along the river path.

No one lived here. Driftwood lay in long ridges along the top of the bank, left there by the last flood. A wolf passed close by them.

'I'm leaving in the morning,' said the girl. 'My dad's got to move on. He owes people money. Business is scratchy.'

Her father ran a scrap barge and spent his time searching the rubbish tips above the mud towns for metal. Not such a respectable job for a citizen.

'I'm going to do something with my life,' she said flatly. 'I don't suppose I'll have a magico friend again.'

'You never used to use that word magico, you used to say Karmidee.'

'I'm just growing up. You know my dad hates me being friends with you. He found out about the raft the other day. I thought he was going to do me in. He says the City would be better off without any of you.'

'If it wasn't for us there wouldn't have been a City at all,' he kicked at a stone on the ground, 'and anyway your mum was a Karmidee, so you're one of us yourself.'

She spun round, very fast, clamped her hands on his

shoulders and pushed her face so close he could smell her skin.

'Maybe she was,' she hissed, 'and maybe I am. You're the only one I've ever told about my mum. She dumped me. I hate her. As far as I'm concerned she never happened. I'm not going to spend my life grubbing about here, poor and hungry and ending up always dazed-out like my dad.'

They were still for a second. Silent. Breathing each other's breath.

'So it's goodbye, scrawny face, and you get out too if you can, except you're too soft. If they need you one day, like you told me, they'll get a surprise. Not exactly the fighting prince, are you? But then none of you people are, really.' And just for that moment she was bleak and tender, like someone old.

Then they both heard a man's voice yelling her name from the river below. A little boat was chugging downstream back towards the mud towns.

'Oh no, that's him now . . .'

The engine stuttered.

'He'll be horrific. He was drinking up in Red Moon this morning, he'll tear you to pieces, get over there out of sight.'

The voice bellowed, 'What are you doing up there, you stupid bitch. I told you to stay at home.'

The boy turned to run but she grabbed his arm.

'Are you sure you couldn't understand it?' she snapped, back to her usual fierce voice. 'You really don't know what it meant?'

'What?'

'The thing about how she can be stopped, the other possible future or whatever?'

Sounds of cursing from the bank. 'If you're with that weird magico kid—'

'I told you,' he said, 'it's like a puzzle, the person who did it wouldn't even have known what it meant—'

'Look again, maybe you missed something, I should have it anyway, I found it, give it to me—'

'Are you crazy? Let me go! He's going to kill me!'

He was fighting to get free and not just because of her famously mad dog father. Up until tonight she had been his best friend. Now that was over and in her head she was already off into her future, without him. He just felt hurt and lonely and very tired. Well this wasn't money, it was something special to do with the Karmidee and he didn't want her to see it again. A pale rainbow of colours flickered for a moment around them, melting into the dark.

Very quick but she saw it.

'Don't get like this. You people are so INTENSE. Just LOOK! Hurry!'

'I don't know what any of it means, the woman with the numbers on her dress, the City, the pile of money, none of it, just LET ME GO!'

He clutched the precious paper through his shirt, colours sparking from his fingers.

She went to grab it just as her mean-faced father, dazed-out as usual on bloodberry juice, came lumbering over the top of the bank.

'YOU get in the boat and YOU, spooky, I'm coming to get YOU right now!'

The boy broke away. With shouts landing around him like spears he ran and stumbled along the bank—

'Stick with your own kind, you skinny little creep—'

His breath hurt. He fell over and his knees were bleeding and he rushed on. At last, behind him, the shouts grew quieter.

He allowed himself to slow to a jog and then, finally, to walk.

The mist had cleared. To one side the river broadened into the muds. On the other there rose up a great web of lights and the moon hung on the black shoulder of a mountain.

As he walked he heard thunder rumble in the distance. The storm came closer. Then there was a jagged stab of lightning and for a moment everything was lit up with savage brightness.

The Raft

The river ran along the edge of a City, a wild panorama of rooftops, steeples, towers, domes and minarets.

Then darkness again and only the silence and the twinkling lights.

And ahead at last he saw the lamps of the mud towns and the river glowing like honey beneath them.

Later, back in the stilt house, he climbed the ladder to his bunk room and hid the parchment under his mattress.

'Nothing to say?' said his father sarcastically, working on a carving. He was disappointed in this son, always reading. He thought he should talk more. Make jokes.

The boy went and sat beside him on the wooden floor.

'Been in a fight? Had an argument with a wolf, or a minotaur, or, let's see now, a dragon perhaps? I thought you were supposed to have a way with creatures. They all love you, don't they?' His father snorted with laughter, 'Looks like you lost your touch. Or perhaps you fell over, running away from something.'

His mother stuck her head through the tattered bead curtain and came back with a bowl of water and a cloth and the boy dabbed at his knees through the holes torn in his trousers.

'You know my mark,' he said suddenly.

They both looked at him.

'Could it be a mistake? I mean, do you think it's really someone else this time and they haven't got a mark, by mistake. And I've got the mark but I'm not really the right one?'

His father struck angrily at his carving. Chips of wood flying.

The boy, as usual, regretted speaking.

But then his mother raised her arms and the bare room became filled with the sounds of the sea. Waves fell on banks of stones and drew back, roaring softly, hissing, softly climbing again. The floorboards gleamed with shells. Gulls cried above them.

'Well I'll be . . .' whispered the father.

'Have I got your attention now?' asked his mother. 'Our son may not be a leader by nature. He doesn't sit around fires endlessly talking about how we might have been if only we had fought harder when they came. We were here for hundreds of years, safe from the Outside. But they came in the end. There is no place in the world they haven't covered with their footprints, the human beings, the Normals. You think we should have fought them. We would have been destroyed.'

'Better than this,' spat his father. 'To be in these slums, poor, our City lost, our powers despised. Self-respect eaten away like rotting flesh—'

The Raft

'You are just like all the other fools, Cornelius, you are like dogs beaten in a fight, creeping around as if that fight was the only fight there would ever be. Who built the Gates that have kept us safe for three hundred years? Without those Gates we'd all be in freak shows on the Outside. In laboratories. Dissected . . . WHO BUILT THOSE GATES?'

No one spoke. The waves rose and fell.

'Well?'

'Araminta . . .' mumbled the father.

'That was what she could do for her people. AND WHEN HIS TIME COMES MY SON WILL FIND A WAY TO HELP HIS PEOPLE TOO.'

She held it a moment longer. The sea, the birds and the blue grey light.

Then she lowered her arms and the scene faded and the room was just the room again.

The girl went back with her father to their barge in Red Moon. He wasn't much help, the father, thumping about and cursing while she did all the work. He slumped down as usual on the bed, knocking over the oil lamp. She heaved the hatch shut. Crept around. Found some food from yesterday. He was worse than ever tonight. Was he finally asleep now?

No. He was staring at her. Awake. Wide-eyed. Very scary.

She stayed quite still.

'You look just like her,' he whispered. 'Same stuck-up snotty bitch eyes.'

She kept her face closed. Made it blank, as she had learnt to do. Giving him nothing to shout at.

From way back inside herself she watched him slide into sleep.

Time had passed. The boy and the girl had grown up.

Dante

It was morning in Parry Street and Albert had been awake all night. He left the flat to go to work just as Alice was arriving to see Otto.

There are no schools in the City of Trees. People choose what they want to learn about, often after they have grown up. The basics however are taught in the children's own homes by women who come especially to do this. They are always cheerful and kind and they are always called Alice or Fumi.

They sat at the kitchen table. Intricate clockwork mobiles, freshly wound by Otto, whirred and chimed and bounced above them. Alice, however, was not easily put off.

'Your science is coming along very well,' she shouted above the noise.

'Did you see Mayor Crumb on telly last night?' asked Otto.

'Yes.'

'Do you think it's all true what he said?'

'Well, Otto, if the Mayor says so then who am I to argue? And what has this got to do with the eight times table that you were going to learn for me?'

'Do you think that the magicos do any harm?'

'Six eights are forty-eight,' said Alice.

Afterwards Otto went down to a place called the Art House in ClockTown.

The Art House was massive and full of different studios and workshops where anyone could go to make things if they wanted.

He was going to meet his friend Dante, they were building a windmill together. The Art House was one of their favourite places.

Dante had got there first.

'My dad's lost his job,' he said at once. 'The mine collapsed where he was working, he was lucky not to get hurt.'

'What's he going to do?'

'What can he do? Mining's the only job he's ever had. We might have to move, maybe over to WorkHouse, it's cheaper there.'

'I'll come and see you.'

'Well, it's a long way. It's these skinking magicos. They should all be locked up. I hate them. All they ever do is hang around looking dazed-out. They're not organized. Don't do steady jobs. Don't do anything useful.'

Dante spat on the floor. Someone working at the next bench looked round at him.

'It might not be them,' said Otto. 'Why should they suddenly do these weird things? They've never done them before. My dad—'

'No danger of HIM losing his job,' continued Dante. 'Nice cushy job he's got, you've got no worries there. It's not like that for us. I'm telling you, Shoes, if it comes to it my dad's prepared to get mean. A lot of the miners are.'

Dante had always called Otto 'Shoes'. It was something to do with toes.

'Let's just go for a walk, Shoes, I don't feel like doing this skinking thing any more.'

'What do you mean, if it comes to it? If it comes to what?'

'I dunno, if it comes to a fight maybe, or something like that.'

They had left the Art House and were walking through the park. In the past they'd wandered for miles together like this, around the parts of the City near to where they lived, looking and talking.

'My dad thinks it could all be made up,' said Otto eventually.

'Haven't you seen the holes? If you don't care about the mines I expect you care about the roads, don't you? It can only be magic. Powerful magic too by all accounts. There's one now, look—'

A hole had opened up next to the Climbing Wood, a series of huge climbing frames that grew by themselves. They had spent whole afternoons there the previous summer. As they walked past now they saw a sign saying 'Danger – Magico Damage'.

'He just thinks it might not be true, that's all,' said Otto.

'I've always said he reads too many books. Or maybe there's another reason. Maybe you've got a magico in your family tree way back. Some people have, you know.'

'Oh no, I don't think so,' said Otto, shocked.

'Just joking, you're far too respectable, up there in Parry Street.'

Otto didn't reply. Dante lived in ClockTown. Most of the miners did.

'Look I've always said you're clever, Shoes, you're a bit small and you don't always say much and your clothes are somewhat lacking in style. But I don't mind any of that because you take your time and you think things out. You've got a good brain. But you don't seem to have got the picture just now. Stop telling people what your dad says, some of the moonstoners would get very agitated about it.'

They walked in silence for a moment and then Dante pointed to some children from ClockTown sitting round one of the fountains.

'I've got to go in a minute. They're all from moonstoning families.'

'I don't know them,' said Otto, his heart sinking.

'No, well you wouldn't, would you, Shoes? Things are difficult at home since this started. We stick together sometimes in the day. If I move I'll let you know, right? My new address.'

He walked off with his easy stride and although Otto stayed awkwardly there, watching him go, he didn't look back.

Zeborah AND Hepzibah

Otto went slowly home.

Hepzibah was in the playpen holding on to the rail. He sat next to her and she grinned and then she simply lifted one leg and then the other into the air behind her, like a swimmer holding on to the side of a swimming pool.

She kicked gently, giggling.

'Mum,' said Otto, not very clearly because something had happened to his voice.

Sounds of washing from the kitchen.

'What is it?' Dolores shouted back.

Hepzibah pulled one hand free.

Otto clung on tight to the other. She felt like a kite, or

one of those balloons that float to the ceiling when you get them home.

'Hepzie's flying,' he said.

Dolores appeared at the sitting room door.

At that moment Hepzie twisted free from Otto's grip and climbed into the air above his head towards the many delicate and tempting mobiles that Mr Hush had made for his wife. She stretched out her small arms, graceful and weightless. She looked beautiful.

'Catch her!' screamed Dolores, running forward and knocking into Otto. But Hepzie was out of reach. She bobbed right up to the high ceiling while her mother and brother crashed around, flailing and yelling.

'She'll fall! She'll fall!' cried Dolores. On the sofa now to try and reach higher.

Zeborah came swaying through from the kitchen with a biscuit in each hand. She looked up at Hepzie and laughed.

Otto knew his sisters well. He grabbed one of Zebbie's biscuits, ran underneath Hepzie and waved it over his head.

'Biscuit,' he shouted.

'Come down, come down, come down!' shouted Dolores.

Hepzie saw the biscuit. She swam down through the air towards it. Her mother seized her by the feet.

Otto stared up at the ceiling; he liked to understand things and now his imagination was full of wires and magnets and

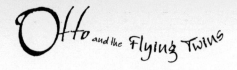

other desperate explanations. Behind him, unseen at first, Zeborah heaved herself onto her father's armchair, stepped off the back and spun slowly into the middle of the room, still sucking the other biscuit.

Above them Mr Hush's loving mobiles were given sudden life by a breeze from outside. Tiny bells chimed. Green, pink and white sugared almonds began to orbit a paper sun.

'The window!' yelled Dolores, who had just seen Zeborah.

AT THE Library

Meanwhile Albert Hush was working in a secluded corner of the quietest part of the basement of the City Central Library. He loved books and he loved his job: it was the only one he had ever wanted to do. He had worked hard for the discreet gold badge he was wearing.

Senior Librarian
Archive of Ancient Documents

And, of course, he knew more about the City's collection of ancient documents than anyone else.

He had one of them in front of him now.

It was just another bit of magico stuff, supposedly of no

interest, but for reasons of his own he was trying to copy it as accurately as possible. He wasn't good at drawing and it was going to be very difficult, especially since it would all have to be done quickly and in secret. There was a pedal-powered photocopying machine but it smudged everything.

A tram rumbled somewhere above.

Then the dusty telephone on the wall began to ring.

Who could have known he was here?

'Mr Hush?'

Of course, it was the Assistant Under Junior Librarian, Miss Fringe. She always seemed to know where he was.

'Er, yes, speaking, I was just checking up on, er, something . . .'

'Your son is on the phone, Mr Hush. Shall I put him through?'

'Please do.'

There were some buzzes and a click and Otto's voice, sounding very strange and very hard to hear, with a background of alarming wailing and banging.

'Is that you, Toe?'

'Dad, Dad can you come home soon?'

'What's wrong? Where's Mummy?'

'She's, she's in the living room.'

Dolores' voice, shouting something that Albert couldn't make out.

'Can I speak to her, Toe? Go and get her.'

A pause. More noises. Was she bathing the twins perhaps? No, not in the living room.

'She's stuck.'

'What?'

'Can you come home early?'

'Is everything all right? What do you mean stuck?'

'She's under the table with Hepzie and Zeb. We're trying to keep them under the table but they're ever so fed up, they want to get out and fly about.'

There was more shouting in the background. He heard Dolores saying to ask him to come home now, at once. Albert held the phone a moment longer while the library basement spun around him.

'Dad? Dad?'

'It's all right,' he whispered. 'I'll come back straight away.'

'Are you feeling a bit poorly then, Mr Hush?' asked Miss Fringe, as she fetched his raincoat. Mr Hush, after all, was almost never off work for any reason.

'Yes, I am a little,' said Albert in a lost sort of voice. 'And there is a problem at home and I must go at once.'

He dived out of one of the side doors of the great library building and started to run awkwardly up the street holding his hat down on his head.

On he went, down the wide pavements under the lime trees. Round this corner and that. Almost hit by a tram at the top of Parry Street. People shouting, horns hooting. At last he was outside Hershell Buildings.

'Are you all right, Mr Hush?' asked Mrs Thudbutton. She didn't care, she was just nosey.

'No,' whispered Albert under his breath, shutting the gate on the ancient lift. It clunked slowly up the stairwell.

At last, the door of the flat.

All was in darkness. The curtains must be drawn. He called hello and was answered by muffled voices. A torch propped up on the floor revealed Dolores and Otto under the table in the living room each holding a sleeping twin. Hours of protest had finally exhausted Hepzibah and Zeborah.

Otto watched his father bend to kiss his mother on the cheek as he often did when he came home. Albert had to crouch down and crawl a little on this occasion, with Dolores being under the table.

THE Burnt Toast

The next morning Otto woke up, remembered that his sisters could fly, jumped excitedly out of bed and ran into the kitchen. It was chaotic in there. His mother was holding Hepzie by the ankle and cramming bread in the toaster with her free hand. Hepzie was giggling and kicking at the air.

Zeb was making little hand prints on the ceiling and the clockwork mobiles lay broken on the floor. Dolores and Albert didn't see Otto at first, what with one thing and another.

'I can't believe you're saying this,' she said angrily. 'Let's just phone Dr Smuggit, why not? Why shouldn't it be a virus? What about that Hopping Virus? I was teaching a modern dance class and two people at the back hopped right out of the window. Good thing we were only on the first floor.

Remember? And that man from downstairs got stuck in a tree, you had to phone the fire brigade. Remember?'

'I just don't think it's a virus,' said Albert quietly.

'OK OK, what about that bug that was going around that made people walk backwards? My mother had it terribly badly. You must remember that. It was definitely a bug. She kept knocking into walls and lampposts and horses and camels—'

'I just don't think it's a bug,' said Albert.

'All right, so maybe it's something they ate. The doctor will know. Maybe they've been having too many vitamins. Maybe it's an allergy. He can test for allergies.'

The toaster was smoking. The toast must have got stuck. Only Otto noticed.

'I don't want to involve the doctor or anyone else,' said Albert.

'Are you saying we do NOTHING?' yelled Dolores, spinning round, accidentally letting go of Hepzie and finding Otto blinking up at her.

'Now look what you've done, Albert, you've upset Ottie,' she added.

'The toaster's on fire,' said Otto.

Albert and Dolores argued all day. Albert, who rarely insisted on anything, did absolutely insist that they didn't tell the doctor, or the Child and Family Mission, or the nice woman at the chemist or any of the other people that Dolores suggested. He said that the doctor wouldn't find anything wrong and the fuss would upset the twins. He said maybe it would wear off in a couple of days.

THE  KARMIDEE TOWER

The next morning Dolores and Otto set off for a walk. The twins were firmly strapped into their double pushchair with the harness provided to stop children falling out.

Dolores strode along, sullen and beautiful in a raspberry coloured dress. Otto had suggested they put the twins on their reins and let them fly like balloons but she didn't seem to think that this was a good idea.

'We don't want anyone to know,' she said. 'Daddy thinks it should be a secret.'

They headed straight for the Boulevard, the grandest and most beautiful shopping street in the whole of the great City of Trees. Otto asked if they could go and sit on one of the benches by the Karmidee Tower, his favourite place. He had often been there with Dante.

Dolores bought everyone an ice cream and as they settled down to eat them, one of the Boulevard Guides came along wearing the traditional crate bird outfit. A small polite crowd of people stood in front of him. (Crate birds are depicted on the City coat of arms. They look a bit like enormous storks.)

'Here we have the legendary Karmidee Tower,' said the Guide, only slightly muffled by his spectacular beak. 'As you can see it is carved stone and made up of animals and birds standing on top of one another. It is extremely tall, much taller than any of the buildings on the Boulevard and it is a pinnacle. It gets thinner as it goes up.'

He had his back to Otto, Dolores and the twins. The twins stared with interest at the zips on his furry orange legs.

'At the bottom we have the three elephants, each as big as a double-decker tram.'

Everyone looked at the elephants. You could walk under the Tower and come out the other side if you wanted.

'Standing on the majestic elephants, of course, we have the rhinoceroses, the hippopotami and then the tigers, the lion king of beasts, the panthers . . .' A long list followed and as it was recited the polite crowd of people leant further and further backwards to try and see further and further up the Tower.

'. . . gorillas, ostriches, flamingos . . . wolves, dingos, ducks . . . domestic cats guinea-pigs hamsters . . .' continued the Guide. And then stopped.

'What is at the top?' asked a member of the crowd politely.

The Guide raised both his large green wings in a dramatic gesture.

'No one knows, ladies and gentlemen, no one knows. The Tower is so high no one can see the top. It is not safe to climb more than three-quarters of the way up because it becomes as thin as a broomstick. We cannot make out clearly even with binoculars. There are trees in the way. We believe there are numerous small rodents and then, possibly, some beetles.'

'Big birdy!' yelled Zeborah, throwing her ice cream in excitement. Some of it stuck to the Guide's tail feathers.

'We'd better go,' hissed Dolores to Otto.

'Big birdy! Big birdy!' cried the twins together. The Guide peered round at them.

'Who built it?' asked another polite person, shouting to make himself heard.

'The Tower is believed to have been the first stone building in our City,' intoned the Guide. 'It is not known now who built it or why. The origin of the name is also a mystery. It is thought to be a coincidence that Karmidee is also the name of the people in Red Moon and TigerHouse. We don't think that the magicos had much to do with such an interesting work of art.'

There was a murmur of laughter from the audience.

Behind the Guide, Dolores was trying to remove her family discreetly from the scene.

'Big birdy! Big birdy!' yelled the twins.

Dolores blushed through her amber skin. They were starting to bounce up and down in their seats alarmingly. The buggy was so light. Could they fly off with it?

'We'll go back the other way, underneath,' she said quickly to Otto.

'It's a very big birdy,' he whispered to Zeborah. 'A very, very, very big birdy.' Much giggling from the buggy.

Then, just as they were right under the Tower with elephants on all sides and the air a bit dank and cold and empty crisp packets lying around, someone stepped out of the dimness and stood in front of them. A man in a long shabby coat.

The buggy thudded to a halt and the twins stopped laughing.

Otto felt his mother grab hold of his collar behind his ear. He stared at the man's face. It was all lined and pitted and, for some reason, familiar.

'Dolores,' said the man in a husky voice, 'I'm Cornelius, Albert's father.' He spoke in the accent of the mud towns. Surely he was a magico.

Otto could tell that she was frightened. She steered round the man, out from under the Tower and into the sunshine on the other side.

The Boulevard Guide and his audience came tramping round the back of the nearest elephant and set off towards the Town Hall. Ice cream dripped here and there from the Guide's tail. His big feet flapped like flippers. Dolores marched her family along behind them, safety in numbers.

'Please listen, Dolores,' said the man, walking alongside. 'I really am Albert's father. He has a small birthmark shaped like a butterfly near his left armpit. He hums a little tune sometimes in his sleep.'

'He told me a long time ago that he didn't want to discuss his family,' she said coldly. 'I have respected that.'

'But you must have wondered. The name and everything.'

'I see nothing unusual in the name Hush,' said Dolores.

Otto saw the man's pasty face go even paler. His small eyes were like chips of stone.

The Guide and his party had come to a halt outside Fozzard's Ice cream Soda Bar. 'Every flavour you could wish for . . . peach, plum, pilchard . . .' he shouted, above the noise of a passing tram.

Dolores stopped too.

'I see nothing unusual in the name Hush,' she repeated.

People streamed past on all sides. Light danced down

through the cherry and chestnut blossom.

'If he has chosen to tell you nothing then that is his affair, he is probably ashamed,' said the man savagely. 'I must ask you to give him a message. I want him to know that if he cares about anything, if he remembers who he is, then they are looking to him now. NOW. IT IS TIME. He is the only one that everyone will trust. More's the pity.'

Dolores stared at him.

Then the man raised his hat and his hair sprang up, very thick and white and for a moment he looked like Otto. He made a small bow and turned away into the crowd.

Dolores swung the buggy round, hitting a woman on the shin, and plunged towards the gleaming shop fronts.

They raced along. Dolores was walking fast. Otto was running. They carved through the crowds like a shark through a shoal of fish.

'Is that man really my grandad?' asked Otto breathlessly.

'I don't know,' snapped Dolores.

She turned sharply into a small square and sat down on a wall.

'Are we going home now, Mum?'

'In a minute,' she said in a puzzled voice. 'I'm just having a little rest.'

* * *

That night, after they thought Otto was asleep, Albert and Dolores had a horrible argument. He couldn't hear everything they said at first because they both kept walking about.

His mother seemed full of hate and hurt.

His father was trying to explain something.

'Why didn't you tell me the truth?' asked Dolores. 'What did you think I would do?'

'I didn't know when to tell you. By the time I knew you well enough to trust you it seemed too late. And what would your parents have said?'

Something indistinct from Dolores.

'Oh yes they do,' said Albert from the living room.

'And surely for the sake of our own children, Al, they don't even know their own . . .' all very muffled.

Otto lay on his back, absolutely still. Moonlight streamed down onto his bed and cast the familiar shadows of his spiders and dragons mobile around the walls of his room.

'There you are,' came his father's voice suddenly, 'that's just the sort of thing people like your father and mother would say. And you're saying it as well. Which proves my point.' He wasn't shouting. Otto couldn't remember him ever shouting really. Dolores was the passionate one.

'Everybody knows they're different, Al, and do weird things and don't have proper jobs. You can always recognize them because they have that accent and can't pronouce the word lemon. They just hang around begging. And now this terrible business about the mines and the holes in the road.'

'For goodness' sake, Dolores!' cried Albert, who might be going to shout now after all, 'you sound just like that idiot Crumb yourself, trotting out all these prejudices. And I can't believe you're judging people by their accents now—'

'I thought we agreed on things like that. And come to think of it, MR HUSH, or whatever your REAL name is, I don't remember YOU ever saying the word LEMON since the day we met. Can you say it properly, Al? The way respectable people do? I SUPPOSE NOT.'

Otto guessed that his father was in the kitchen. He heard something that could be the fridge door. Whatever Albert said next was lost among the milk and yogurts.

Hepzie started crying.

'You're a fake! It's all been lies! How can I believe anything you say now?' shouted Dolores. 'And whatever was all this he said about NOW, and IT IS TIME, whatever does all THAT mean?'

Otto flung himself out of bed and opened the door. He stared at their shocked faces. Then he pushed past and went into the twins' room. He was too small to reach down and get them out of their cots but this didn't matter because they were flying round anyway, half asleep, crying mournfully, knocking into each other.

Immediately Albert and Dolores started hurrying about, the twins were comforted and Otto was given a cup of milk, a biscuit and a piece of apple, none of which he particularly wanted.

When all this was over Dolores took him back to his room and made a lot of fuss plumping up his pillows and straightening his duvet.

Meanwhile Otto looked out of the window and saw a black unicorn with a silver horn trotting past down the middle of the street.

The clip-clop of its hooves echoed off the buildings.

Then, not far behind, there came a small piece of carpet flying a few feet off the ground with a little girl sitting in the middle of it. It all happened quite fast and he didn't have time to notice much but he did see that she was dressed in a patchwork of blacks and greens and her long pale hair streamed behind her.

'Get back into bed then, Ottie,' said Dolores, 'we're all going to sleep now.'

The next morning at breakfast everything continued to be strange and horrible. Otto dropped his toast on the floor by accident. No one said anything. In fact his parents didn't speak to each other at all at first. As he was putting his coat on Albert reached down and tweaked Otto's nose.

'I saw a unicorn,' said Otto.

'Really?' said Albert.

'There are no such things as unicorns, Ottie,' said Dolores.

'But it went down the street, right outside.'

'You were half-asleep.'

'No I wasn't. It was black with a shiny horn.'

'If he says he saw one then perhaps he did,' said Albert, 'there used to be plenty around.'

'There are no such things as unicorns,' said Dolores. 'The Mayor was giving an interview about all that sort of thing the other day. If you did see something then it must have been a horned horse.'

Albert let out a hiss of breath, 'You aren't serious?'

'Of course, that's what they're called, horned horses. And if you see one you're supposed to report it so the police can catch it and remove its horn.'

Otto, forgotten, looked under the table for the toast. It had fallen jam side down.

For some reason Albert seemed especially horrified about the horned horses. 'May butterflies fly,' he said softly. 'This is like murder, this is very very wrong.'

'Oh really, Albert, what rubbish. A horse with a horn is deformed and it is kinder to remove the horn to make it like other horses. Now not being truthful with your family, letting your children grow up to believe that they are one thing

when really they are another. To believe they are respectable when really—'

'They are PERFECTLY ALL RIGHT!' yelled Albert.

Under the table Otto had discovered that the jammy side of the toast was covered in little bits of dirt and hair and things. It was his fault, of course, for dropping it.

'I'm talking about blood, Albert, the blood that runs in their veins. YOU are not who I thought you were until yesterday. And neither are THEY. Can you deny that? You can't deny that, can you?'

Otto saw his father's feet march out of the room. The corridor creaked as it always did and the front door clicked shut. His mother's feet walked right round the table and he heard her sniffing.

'I'm going to wake the twins, Otto,' she said after a moment. 'They'll never go to sleep tonight if we don't get them up soon.'

Alone now, Otto sat quietly in his cave of chair legs and tablecloth. He wished he could stay there and have some more toast and pretend he was a really little kid again. He thought perhaps he'd like to live under there for a long time.

THE Hush Family AT HOME

If your sisters suddenly learn to fly, then it is obvious that things are going to be different and adjustments will have to be made. It is a time for a family to pull together. To act as a team. To unite in the face of this interesting challenge. The Hush family failed to do any of these things.

Albert and Dolores continued to argue a lot at first. Then they seemed to lose the energy and just became quieter and quieter. Albert spent long hours at the library and often worked at the weekends. No time now to build mobiles with Otto.

Dolores stopped looking after herself like she used to do. She wore the same clothes day after day. Her beautiful black hair stuck out in all directions. She did the housework very

bitterly and sometimes she phoned her mother and cried.

They couldn't have the electric lights on because Hepzie liked tugging at the lampshades on the ceiling. The curtains had to be drawn and the windows closed to prevent them flying straight into the glass or, most terrifying of all, simply pottering out into the air over Parry Street. Going out was a worry. No one must know. The flat became like a prison.

For a while Otto did a lot to look after his little sisters. He was the one who made them their breakfast (mashed sardines followed by ice cream) and played with them. If there was a problem he could usually sort it out. The sight of tiny children spinning through the air didn't upset him. It was fun. It was almost as good as being able to fly himself.

Meanwhile the twins enjoyed the high ceilings of the flat. They bounced from wall to wall in the wide corridor and they found soft silvery dust on top of the kitchen cupboards.

'Ottie come too!' they called.

But he was solid and earthbound. He could only run along below shouting advice and warnings, trying to protect them.

Otto AND Mab

Midsummer was coming. Down on Parry Street the Hush family regretted their problem with windows.

At night Otto's was the only one that was opened wide. Dolores left the heavy velvet curtains open too.

It was a tall sash window, almost from the ceiling to the floor.

Sometimes he went and sat and looked down at Parry Street for a while.

He hadn't given up hope that he would one day see another horned horse or maybe the extraordinary little girl flying along on her scrap of carpet.

So far nothing had happened.

Then something did.

First the little girl came hurtling past. She was much higher and going much faster than before. She was as high as the tops of the lime trees. Her carpet rocked and bounced through the air. As she went by he saw her grip the front edge with both hands.

Something horrible was chasing her on the road.

It looked like a street-cleaning machine, except it moved a bit faster. There was a member of the Normal Police standing on the back. There was a crack and a glimmer, like a snake in the air. The policeman had fired a net that opened, just missing the girl and the carpet. He got ready to fire again.

Then the carpet suddenly climbed even higher, lurched round in a great curve, skimmed the treetops opposite and came back towards Otto, bumping through the air, dipping from side to side so sharply, surely she would fall off.

He pushed the window open as far as he could and leant out, waving his arms.

The little carpet was losing height. She was curled over now and it was almost wrapped around her.

She had seen him.

She was plunging straight at him.

At the last moment he jumped sideways on to the bed and she came crashing into the room.

* * *

He quickly pulled the curtains closed and put out the bedside light. At first he could just see shapes.

'Help me!' commanded a voice from the floor. 'There's a spider!'

She had hit the spider and dragon mobile and was all tangled up in it.

'It's not real,' he said and knelt beside her and began to pull the spiders and snakes away from her face.

He could see a bit more now.

She didn't smile.

And outside the machine went past on the road, and a voice, carried on the night air, said, '. . . could be on any of these roofs, probably crashed, the way it was going. Did you see a kid at a window, Mr Six? What was he doing? Can you see a light up there anywhere?'

They stayed still as the sound of the engine died away down the long street.

'Are you all right?' asked Otto.

'I think so,' she said. 'Get my mat.'

Otto picked up the carpet, which was crumpled against the bottom of his bedroom door. She pulled it out of his hands and began smoothing it and examining it, holding it very close to her face.

At first it just looked mottled to Otto, a muddy pattern of blues and browns. Then he realized it was covered in a design

of tiny butterflies, all different shapes and shades.

'Is it OK?' he asked after a while.

She didn't answer. Just kept feeling the carpet and peering at it, inch by inch.

Otto noticed that she had a tattoo around her ankle, faint and fine like a spider's web. And her clothes were dirty.

'So who are you?' she asked at last, cradling the carpet on her knees. She had a low, husky voice.

'I'm Otto,' whispered Otto.

'Otto,' she repeated.

'Yes.' He raised his finger to his lips. Not a good idea to wake anybody up. She began to whisper too. 'Why did you help me, Otto? You took a big risk.'

'That thing was going to get you.'

'So what do you care? Maybe you're going to hand me over.'

'Who to?'

She was watching him all the time.

'To the Normal Police, of course. The Normies.'

'Never,' said Otto fiercely.

She went on watching him.

'You're very young,' she said, 'aren't you?'

He didn't reply. He was forever being told that he was small for his age. Well, she was rather small herself.

'You do know what the Normal Police are, do you?'

'I know they're blaming magicos for a lot of things. My dad thinks it's wrong. Live and let live, he says.'

He thought it best not to quote Dolores, who seemed to have quite a different view.

She didn't give any sign that she'd even heard him but she did begin to look a little round the room. The other mobiles were undamaged, the crate birds, the dragons and the flying dinosaurs. Made by Albert and Otto together in another lifetime.

'I'm not really scared of spiders,' she said.

'No, oh no,' said Otto.

'Mab,' she said. And held out her hand.

Otto shook it, wondering if this was what he was supposed to do. He had never shaken hands with another child before. Her hand felt small, cool and bony and she wore rings.

'You took a big risk there,' she said again, 'and you're wearing red and white striped pyjamas, your eyes are green, your skin is brown with black freckles. Your hair is in locks. It's white. As white as bones.'

'How can you see all that in the dark?'

'Just showing off, Mr Normal.'

'Can you all do that?'

'No, of course not, people are different. You don't know much, do you? What do you think magicos are like anyway, what do you know about us?'

The word seemed even uglier than usual now he was talking to a real magico, the first one he'd ever properly met.

'Well, er, they can do tricks, making things change colour, turning drinks to ice . . .' He'd seen all these done on the Boulevard. He trailed off. Although he'd seen magicos in the street all his life, begging or busking or selling things or just dazed-out on bloodberry juice, he didn't really know what made them magicos at all. Grown-ups didn't talk about it.

'Yeah, we make good magicians, we can get some little tricks together to entertain dummies like you,' said Mab. 'But that's just games. The thing that makes us different from you is our energy. It isn't all inside us. That's the only way I can explain it to someone like you. Like, some of us, when we're angry or very upset, all these colours appear around us. Not really under our control. Some people can move things, or change things from hot to cold. And it's not just ourselves. We can put energy into things. Like the City. All the magic that you people seem to think is Normal. Weather in different places, musical trees. Moving statues. The hat snatcher.'

'What about seeing in the dark?'

'I use my eyes as lamps, Mr Normal. Watch, I'll have a look at your ceiling, not that I think there will be anything of interest up there—'

He watched as she turned her face upwards. Her eyes

glowed. A very faint soft silvery light. And across the ceiling, two tiny beams dancing.

She turned her gaze on him and the lights swept across his face like moths and she laughed—

'You should see your expression. Close your mouth, something might fly into it.'

'What would have happened if they'd caught you?' he asked quickly.

'There's a curfew. They'd have stolen my mat and then taken me back to the mud towns. After a little chat. They're very interested in our powers all of a sudden, after trying to make us ashamed of them for hundreds of years. And they're offering people money to go and be in some sort of magic show. Nobody wants to, though. They're particularly interested in kids. They're looking for ones that can fly. Without mats I mean.'

'Ones that can fly . . .' whispered Otto.

'Didn't you know about that either? It's one of our legends, that sometimes kids can fly. Really little kids. It's a joyful thing.'

He was trying to sound casual. 'Why are they looking for children who can fly?'

'Relax. Look, they say it used to happen, before the Karmidee were so crushed the way they are now. Little children being able to fly just because they're little and

excited about everything. That hasn't happened for ages and it's very rare . . . Just imagine though, it would be amazing, wouldn't it?'

Otto didn't need to imagine how amazing it would be. He couldn't speak.

'Stop panicking,' she said in her cold way. 'No one is going to arrest *you* if you're out at night. It's kids like me they're after. Kids from Red Moon and TigerHouse. Not just kids either. Any Karmidee, all the other kinds too.'

'What others?' he managed to ask.

'Well there's different sorts of Karmidee. It's just an old word for magical energy. There's dammerung, very few nowadays, and multiples, and artists and widges, they can do real magic but they need cats to help them. They mainly live in the City itself. Then some people are good with creatures.'

'Creatures like dragons?' blurted Otto.

'Sure. And then there are the creatures themselves, dragons, unicorns, wolves, troll-trees—'

'Are the widges, or whatever you said, the only ones who live in the City?' Otto's mind was racing.

'Oh no, there's the sleepers as well. That's what we call Karmidee who go and live in the City and get jobs and pretend to be Normals. They just decide to disappear. It's difficult but some people reckon it's the only way to do anything with

64

your life. We have a King, would you believe, and he's a sleeper somewhere right now.'

'A king?'

'Our kings and queens are different from the ones in your history books, they don't fight battles and have jewels and all that. They're chosen by a birthmark. When they grow up they're supposed to do something for our people. It is a question of honour.'

'Like what?'

For the first time since she'd come crashing in his window she seemed embarrassed and reluctant to explain.

'OK, so they haven't done much for a lot of years now and most of them have ended up dazed-out and useless like most of the rest of us. But your sort of kings and queens can be like that too. And at least we don't have to give ours money, or palaces, or whatever. We don't have leaders and mayors and all that.'

'So why doesn't your King do something about what's happening now?'

He saw her shrug in the darkness. Wished he could light his own eyes and find the expression in hers.

A silence chilled the room.

THE Whispering Park

Hepzie cried sleepily through the wall.

'Is anyone going to come in here?' whispered Mab.

He shook his head.

'Big family, huh?'

He held up four fingers and a thumb.

More crying. Floorboards creaking. Dolores' voice, soft.

'Want to come for a ride on the mat?'

He just stared at her.

'Too scared,' she smiled. 'Don't worry, you people are soft, we know that.'

'I'm not scared,' Otto gabbled, 'I've never been on a flying carpet. I might fall off, or we might get chased by that thing. Why are you flying about anyway? With that thing after you?'

Mab was already at the window, looking down Parry Street through the gap in the curtains.

'I hate them,' she said quietly. 'They won't stop me flying over my own City. There's three of us with mats. We fly everywhere. That's how they start to take away the being from you, by making you afraid.'

Otto, who had never been so afraid, stood by her and looked out too.

She opened the curtains and picked up the carpet. It was definitely the smallest carpet Otto had ever seen. The more he thought about riding on it, the smaller it seemed to be. She let go and it hovered by the open window.

'Perhaps it needs a rest after the crash and should only really have one person on it,' he suggested hopefully.

A moment later the carpet had two people on it and was progressing slowly and smoothly over the trees as it went down Parry Street.

His eyes were tightly shut.

'Stop squeezing me so much,' she hissed at him.

He was sitting behind her with his arms around her waist.

'Can't we go any slower?'

'If we go any slower we'll just go downwards. Look, I'll show you your City. I bet you've never seen it properly before.'

To Otto's horror and despair the carpet began to climb higher. They were going away from the Boulevard, past the dim outline of the Karmidee Tower.

'The oldest parts are HighNoon and SteepSide.' The whole carpet rocked as Mab let go with one hand, presumably to point somewhere. 'It's those lights over there on the side of BlueRemembered. That's where the wool bandits were. The Mook family are still there, they run a wool shop now but they're descended from the original wool bandits.'

Otto, who had no idea what a wool bandit was, made no comment.

'And over there is The Heights, where the rich people are. And of course down there you've got The Gardens. Over there is WorkHouse, not very nice, and Clock-Town . . .'

How high were they for goodness' sake? Otto imagined the City shrinking to the size of his palm below him.

Whatever happened he would never ever go on a flying carpet again.

Mab was continuing to tell him about all sorts of places that were too far away to show him tonight. The Vineyards. WaterTown, all canals. The moonstone mines, Guido's Beach, PasturesGreen, Greenwood.'

'I'd like to go home now,' said Otto faintly.

Too faint for Mab to hear, it seemed.

'I know a brilliant place to take you,' she exclaimed suddenly, and the carpet tilted as they swept round to the west and began a gentle descent.

Sometime later, a very, very long time as far as Otto was concerned, they landed with a soft bump somewhere.

'Isn't it beautiful seeing the City lights and the river in the moonlight?' said Mab.

'Oh, yes,' said Otto fervently.

'You can open your eyes by the way,' she added, laughing. 'We really are on the ground.'

They were in some sort of park. Otto had never seen it before. They had landed inside the gates which were tall and padlocked shut. Grass had grown up around them.

Then he jumped in fright. There was a faint sound of metal clattering on metal. Normal Police?

'It's OK,' said Mab, 'come on, I'll show you.' She had rolled up her carpet under her arm.

'So what was that?' croaked Otto casually.

'This is the Whispering Park,' said Mab. 'I thought you'd like it because you've got all those mobiles. This place is full of things like that.'

A giant mobile, apparently made out of metal birds, loomed up in the moonlight.

At first Otto couldn't see how it was suspended. Then he

realized that it wasn't. The birds were just floating.

As Mab walked past they began to circle very slowly flapping their rusty wings.

'Imagine what it was like when it was new,' said Mab. 'All shiny.'

They walked deeper into the park. Tall craggy trees stood at intervals on the mossy grass. And between them floated fantastical creatures, dancing children, mermaids drifting through waves of twisted wire, crate birds, clumsy as ever, gently colliding and parting again.

'I didn't think you'd know about this,' she said smugly. 'It's a secret place, only Karmidee come here.'

They were coming towards a mobile made of hundreds of tiny metal fish.

'It's a shoal,' she said. 'They all face one way, sometimes they all turn very fast, not often though, it won't happen now—'

Otto, who noticed things, noticed that she suddenly seemed different.

He wandered underneath and looked up.

At that moment the fish did all turn very fast just like a shoal in the sea.

'It must be to do with the wind,' said Otto.

Mab stared at him with a strange expression and then she walked on a little way without speaking.

'The person who designed this place was arrested a couple of weeks ago,' she said eventually.

'Arrested! Why?' exclaimed Otto.

'They don't stop to chat,' said Mab dryly. 'So I don't know.'

'You mean you were there?'

He saw her face freeze over. Two stabs of light from her eyes. Very quick and cold.

'I didn't say that, Mr Normal.'

He gave up.

They'd come to another open space. A towering pagoda disappeared up into the dark and a sign said, 'Tea and Ice cream'.

She unrolled her carpet.

He had planned to announce that he would walk back, even though he was sure they were many miles from Parry Street and he had no idea of the way. But the thought of her superior smile silenced him.

She took him straight home. She had to go back herself, she said, or her parents would worry. She practically tipped him in through his window.

'I can't come in,' she whispered, as the carpet hovered unsteadily. 'Take this. Use it if you ever want to see me. It eats cabbage and stuff like that.'

She threw something past him onto the bed, pulled at the

fringe of the carpet and was off into the dawn before Otto could protest.

He searched around on the bed and found a small box with holes in the lid. Inside there was a bright green beetle. For a moment he was just very pleased that she had given him something. Then he thought that perhaps it was a joke. Then, very tired, he crept to the kitchen for some cabbage.

GRANNY Culpepper

Granny Culpepper was Dolores' mother, Otto's grandmother. She was short and tough-looking like some sort of bush you can grow anywhere. She frowned all the time as if her face might fall off if she smiled and she lived with Grandpa Culpepper in a big house on The Heights.

Since everything had changed Dolores phoned her almost every day.

Then, one afternoon when Otto and the twins were having a particularly good game blowing soap bubbles (almost any game is better when you can fly) Granny Culpepper arrived with her suitcase. It had all been arranged, apparently. She had left Grandpa Culpepper with instructions to phone her every night and she had come to help. Her cat Shinnabac

came with her. He was big and sleepy and his fur came off everywhere.

'They like ice cream for breakfast,' explained Otto. 'Hepzie has strawberry and Zeb has chocolate.'

'Do they indeed,' said Granny Culpepper.

'Yes, and mashed bananas and yoghurt for lunch. They have it in the bathroom so that they can fly about while they're eating it.'

'Otto,' said Granny Culpepper, 'your sisters can't fly, it isn't possible. They are dancing. Your mother and theirs is, after all, a professional teacher of dance. We have many dancers in our family.'

Zeborah danced above Granny Culpepper's head at that moment and threw a mug of water over her.

Otto stood with his mouth open. Not because of the water, that happened all the time.

'Fetch me a towel,' said Granny Culpepper, dripping sternly.

Later he tried to discuss it. His father, most unusually, was home early and playing with the twins. Dolores was in the bathroom and Granny Culpepper was cooking in the kitchen.

'But they CAN fly, Granny,' he said. 'That's why we have the windows shut and everything and this screen to keep them out of the kitchen and all the mobiles have been moved, except the ones in my room, and the ones that got broken—'

'Not another word, Otto,' said his granny sharply.

Albert had come into the room, holding each daughter by an ankle.

'I don't want to hear any more about it,' she went on. 'They are not flying. They are dancing. You are too young to understand. And I'll get their meals in future. Ice cream for breakfast, whatever next.'

Otto ran out of the kitchen and into his room. Behind him he heard Zeb calling, 'Ottie play! Ottie play!'

A moment later his door creaked open. It was Albert. He came and sat on the bed.

'They can fly, can't they, Dad?' whispered Otto.

'It certainly looks like it, yes.'

'So why does Granny say they're only dancing? People don't dance on ceilings. Do they?'

'Half a pound of TUPPENNY RICE,' boomed Granny Culpepper's voice from the living room. A sound of something being dropped from a height. It took a while to get used to looking after the twins.

Albert looked very tired.

'Tiny children being able to fly is a bit unusual, Otto. It's not really respectable.'

'You mean it might be something that would happen to magico children,' said Otto carefully.

There was a small pause.

'Well, yes.'

'That's why we keep them hidden in the flat, isn't it, because the Normies are looking for children who can fly?'

Albert looked at him sharply.

'Are they? Especially? How did you hear that?'

'I thought you knew that, Dad. I thought that was why they're such a secret. And is it true that a few of the Karmidee live in the City pretending to be Normal and they're called sleepers?'

The door burst open and Granny Culpepper came staggering into the room. She needed someone to help her to get peanut butter out of her eyes, ears, hair and nose. It was urgent.

Afterwards Albert rushed off to the library, even though it was a Sunday, and stayed there until after Otto had gone to sleep.

Honeybun Nicely

By the time Otto woke up the next morning Albert had already gone to work.

Granny Culpepper made it clear to Otto that he was no longer needed to look after the twins. Every time he tried to help or to explain how she might do something she always said she could manage. Children love nursery rhymes, rice pudding and porridge. Her head seemed to be full of rules and regulations.

'Ottie play . . .' called the twins, who missed him.

But it was no good.

Dolores, seeing the situation, sent him to do some shopping.

He went down Parry Street, crossed the Boulevard, and

made his way to Dealer's Square to get the vegetables. There was a problem with the road just there, another hole had appeared during the night.

The last thing he had to do was get the twins some more cereal bowls (the third ones in a week). That meant going back to the Boulevard and then along to the famous china shops.

He never made it.

Things began to happen after he decided to sit down for a rest by the Karmidee Tower.

He and Dante had often seen fire-eaters and acrobats performing there. No sign of them now. No one begging either. Not even anyone selling cheap clocks out of a suitcase.

A woman came and sat down next to him. She wore a perfume that Dolores sometimes wore and the smell of it made him feel sad.

When he saw the front of her newspaper he felt worse.

IS YOUR NEIGHBOUR A MAGICO?

POLICE BELIEVE THAT MANY MORE MAGICOS ARE LIVING SECRETLY IN THE CITY.

THEY SEEM NORMAL. ARE THEY

DANGEROUS? HOW CAN WE SPOT THESE FAKERS?

FIVE THINGS TO LOOK FOR:

Otto sneaked a bit closer, trying to see what the five things were.

POINT ONE – DOESN'T KNOW ALL THE WORDS OF THE NEW CITY ANTHEM, 'WE'RE SO NORMAL.'

POINT TWO – LIKES DIGGING, MAY POSSESS A SHOVEL.

POINT THREE – DID NOT VOTE FOR MAYOR CRUMB AT THE LAST ELECTION.

Otto could feel sweat starting to prick in his hair.

Two Normal Police came under the Tower, and stopped a thin bow-legged man who had been feeding a crate bird with bananas.

Otto couldn't quite see POINT FOUR.

The man was looking in all his pockets, presumably for his identity papers. The crate bird stood nearby on one leg, holding a banana in the other foot and peeling it with its beak.

The Normies looked very familiar. They reminded him a

lot of the ones who had been driving the street-cleaning machine that had been trying to catch Mab.

The woman slowly folded her newspaper and, also slowly, put it in her bag. Then she just sat very still, watching what was happening.

Then suddenly the whole scene changed.

In the high summer there is a sudden strong wind, known as the hat snatcher, which seems to come from nowhere, plunges and eddies and spins down the Boulevard, reaches the other end and stops. Although inconvenient, it is also appreciated because it keeps the Boulevard pleasantly fresh even on the most sultry, sticky days. This was the reason it was created. It is a very unusual thing, which, of course, everyone thinks is Normal.

Just as the thin man was handing his identity papers to one of the Normies the first hat snatcher of the season blasted round the side of the Tower. The papers flew out of the Normie's hand. The crate bird was blown over, still resolutely clutching the banana. A man who had been walking under the Tower came chasing after his hat, and several helpful people ran off to try and catch it, all getting in each others' way.

The papers shot straight over to Otto and the woman and the Normies came straight after them.

In the tiny moment before they arrived Otto heard the woman swearing in a whisper.

Then the papers wrapped themselves around his feet.

'I'll have those if you don't mind,' said the Normie, as if Otto had stolen them.

Otto bent down and picked them up. He was absolutely sure now that this was the same Normie who had looked up from the street-cleaning machine and said, 'Did you see a kid at a window, Mr Six?'

He handed the papers over.

'You seem a bit tense, young man,' said the Normie.

Out of the corner of his eye Otto saw that the woman was getting something out of her bag.

'Don't I know you from somewhere?'

The other Normie came over, holding the man they had been talking to by the collar of his patched-up coat.

'Yeah, I know, you're the kid who was at that window when we was trying to get hold of that little magico trash that got away. You've got rather unusual hair, haven't you. Distinctive. Memorable, wouldn't you say, Mr Eight? Look at him, he's all wound up . . .'

Otto stared. There was no way he could run. The Normie was practically standing on him.

Then the woman opened the thing she'd got out of her handbag, which was a little pocket mirror. Surely not going to put lipstick on NOW.

'Got any ID on you?' asked the Normie.

'He's too young for ID,' said the other one.

The woman held the mirror up, nestling neatly in the palm of her hand. Otto caught a glimpse of her deep blue eye in the glass, she was looking at him. Then she tilted it a tiny bit, away from her and towards the Boulevard beyond the Normies.

'Let's take both these down to the station,' said the Normie who was holding the thin man.

'Good day's work,' said the other one.

'And what exactly is your work?' asked the woman, staring very hard into her mirror.

'We're tidying up, citizen, getting all the rubbish off the streets,' said one of the Normies and they both laughed.

'Excellent,' said the woman, 'there's some over there, look . . .'

For some reason everyone looked.

A huge pile of something had appeared on the pavement. It was amazing and multi-coloured and it was writhing as if it was alive. Flags and children's windmills fluttered and spun on the top, mask-like faces of animals and birds formed and dissolved on the surface. Sparkling shoes cascaded down the sides. Dancing shoes, elegant high heeled shoes, dainty slippers with fluffy bits on. Then some fruit. Pineapples. Oranges. Melons.

The Normies, the man who was being arrested, Otto and everyone else in sight froze with astonishment.

Otto felt the woman pull at his arm.

No one else was moving.

'Come on,' she whispered. 'It won't last very long, it's just a shopping list.'

She grabbed the thin man by the hand and tried to pull him away. But the Normie still had hold of his jacket.

'Oh, for goodness' sake!' she said, and reached up and tugged the thin man this way and that until his jacket came off and was left hanging from the Normie's hand.

'Hurry up, the pair of you!'

She had to drag them away. It was very, very hard not to just stand and stare.

The last thing Otto saw as he was marched backwards under the Tower was an impressive shower of what looked like tiny sugar cake decorations.

The thin man took the woman's hand and held it to his lips. 'Madame,' he began, 'I am forever in your debt, if ever you should—'

'I know,' she said. 'That is a promise made with honour and accepted with gratitude, now please hurry.' She was the opposite of the thin man, all curves. Even her hair was curvy.

The man hurried away.

There were shouts now and running feet.

'It's worn off,' said the woman.

She pushed Otto towards the nearest way out of sight,

some revolving doors. Back in the chaos at the Karmidee Tower the crate bird discreetly began to unpack the forgotten bag of shopping.

THE *Impossible* COMMITTEE

Otto found himself in Banzee, Smith and Banzee, the biggest, smartest and most expensive department store on the Boulevard, right next to the Town Hall.

He dodged through the hat department and down the first stairs he saw. Down past the kitchen section. Another floor. Basement. Toilets.

He knew now he'd been stupid. He should have done anything rather than go downwards like this. This way he was going to get trapped.

There were three doors. Gentlemen, Ladies and Staff Only — No Admittance.

The one marked Gentlemen opened and a man came out dressed in the extremely smart uniform of the Banzee, Smith

and Banzee Security Guards. (This involved a ridiculously large amount of gold braid.)

'Looking for something, sonny?' he asked, in a not very friendly voice.

'I'm just going in here,' said Otto, going past him, 'someone's waiting for me upstairs.'

He went into the toilets. An enormous place with marble floors and copper taps.

This was madness.

He went back out again, heard a voice that he thought might be one of the Normies saying something like, '. . . did he go down here?' He jumped through the door marked Staff Only – No Admittance.

He was in some sort of boiler room.

The walls were brick and the floor stone. As he went further in, he felt the thump of engines all around him. Huge pipes ran in all directions, some above his head.

Behind him the door opened.

It probably wasn't the Normies. But by this time Otto couldn't stop running. He saw a hole in the wall. Some sort of heating shaft? The grille had been taken off, he could see it on the floor, the heating was off for the summer. In fact it looked as if the grille had been repainted. He heaved himself up and climbed in. He could fit in OK as long as he crawled. So he just kept crawling.

He didn't have to go far before he came to a junction. The shaft stretched away to both the left and right. There were dim patches of light, presumably coming from the grilles that let the warm air out of the shaft and into different parts of the shop.

Still scared and with no plan whatsoever Otto turned left. He crawled on briskly.

Then the shaft began to climb upwards and he reached another junction and turned right and after that he stopped remembering if and where he had turned right or left and just thought about how much he wanted to stand up straight.

He decided that he must now be level with the ground floor of the shop. For some reason the grilles were now on the other side of the shaft. He stopped at each one and rattled it quietly, but they were all fixed tight. And anyway, it didn't seem to be the ground floor of the shop after all, in fact it didn't look much like Banzee, Smith and Banzee any more. All he could see through the grilles was a succession of small rather grand-looking rooms with nobody in them and tables and lots of chairs.

It was a horrible feeling. If he tried to go back to the boiler room he'd have to crawl backwards. How long would that take? Anyway he didn't know the way.

He even thought of shouting for help; but the thought of the Security Guard outside the toilets stopped him. They'd

probably send for the Normal Police.

Yet another empty room. He reached to rattle the grille and froze. The door was opening. Mayor Crumb came into the room.

Otto tried to shuffle backwards.

The Mayor looked towards the grille.

Otto didn't dare to move again. Instead, after a moment, he had the idea of very slowly easing himself from kneeling to lying down. As he did this, sending waves of relief through his back and knees, he saw Mayor Crumb unpack his briefcase on the table. Papers, files, a packet of biscuits, an alarm clock, a box of tissues.

Then, unexpectedly, a quick flick through his pale sticky hair with a comb, using a hand mirror from his pocket.

The door opened and a very singular-looking woman walked in. She wore a long raincoat. Her face was like armour and her eyes looked out from behind it.

It was the woman who had been on the television. Councillor Elfina Crink, Minister for Modernization.

She looked swiftly round the room and Otto shuddered in fear.

He realized now, of course, these rooms were in the Town Hall. It must share a heating system with Banzee, Smith and Banzee. He had always heard that the whole city was riddled with tunnels and passageways and even underground rooms, if you knew where to find them.

'I'm extremely busy,' said Elfina to the Mayor. 'I hope you've got a good reason.'

Her voice went well with her armoured face.

The Mayor fumbled with his papers.

'You said it was to do with a new committee,' she prompted him.

'Yes, my love, it is, it is, all my own idea and just for you.'

'Don't call me love here.'

'But we're alone, angel.'

'Not that either. None of that. It's private.'

The Mayor made to snatch her hand but she snatched it away faster.

'Just get on with it.'

He didn't seem to notice how nasty she was being.

'You plan to modernize the City and get the magicos off the streets and into proper jobs and make everything respectable,' he said.

'What about it?'

'Well, I was thinking the other day. There's quite a few things here that are probably different from the Outside. Perhaps even not respectable, perhaps even, strictly speaking, Impossible. Perhaps things which, in some way, are a bit, well, magical.'

'Like what?'

'Well, that's what this new committee is for, you see. I've called it the Impossible Committee and we're working on putting together an Impossible List.'

Otto could tell that the woman wasn't pleased.

'There's nothing Impossible in the City, it's perfectly Normal, just like the Outside,' she snapped. 'My plan is to keep the City exactly as it is and simply provide employment for the magico element.'

The Mayor trundled hopefully on.

'Well I want to help you make things better by ridding us of anything that might be connected with them. Everyone knows that they may have had some part in building this City long ago. Just a small, primitive part before the Normal people came and made it what it is today. Stands to reason some things about it aren't totally Normal. It's just a question of working out what they are. Now, I thought of interviewing some tourists—'

Elfina breathed in sharply.

'. . . but then I decided to do it properly and send a couple of people off to the Outside to gather information in a scientific manner. They're reporting back to the meeting today. After all we do know there are no magicos on the Outside, don't we, so it must be free from their primitive influences.'

'How did they go?' she asked quickly. 'How did they come back?'

'What do you mean, dearest?'

'How did they leave the City? How did they get back in?'

'Well, through the Gates I imagine, my cherry pie. There is no other way.'

Otto could tell that Elfina was trying to calm down. She patted the Mayor's hand, like someone patting a dog.

'Of course there isn't, my darling,' she whispered.

Behind them the door opened again and the members of the Impossible Committee started to arrive.

In the heating shaft Otto managed to look at his watch. He was due home with the shopping about now.

'Good afternoon, fellow councillors,' said Mayor Crumb, when everyone had assembled. 'I am pleased to welcome the Minister for Modernization, Councillor Elfina Crink.'

Once more Councillor Crink lasered around the room from behind her face. Everyone became still.

The Mayor beamed.

'Councillor Trim and Councillor Tapper are going to talk to us about the Outside. Please, Councillors. We need to know what it is like there so that we can make our Impossible List.'

Otto could only see the two travellers from the back as they stood up, shuffling papers.

'Your most worshipful honourable rather important Lord Mayorness,' began Councillor Trim, his voice trembling, 'we intended to follow your instructions, we will go tomorrow first thing . . .'

Councillor Tapper nudged him.

'We saw a boy juggling with sixty-four bicycle wheels on the Boulevard, that seemed Impossible. But we're not sure.'

'Perhaps you could clarify this,' said the Mayor patiently.

A long pause.

'We had some ice cream,' said Councillor Tapper.

Another pause.

'Are you telling me that you haven't been yet?'

Yet another pause. The Mayor's forehead twinkled with extra sweat.

'I really don't remember you telling us to go anywhere,' whispered Councillor Trim miserably.

'ARREST THESE FOOLS,' boomed the Mayor, making everyone jump, including Otto who banged his elbow smartly on the shiny wall of the shaft.

The Mayor produced a whistle from his pocket and blew it so hard that spit showered out of the other end. A woman blocked her ears.

Otto understood the problem. The plan to impress Elfina Crink had gone all wrong.

The Impossible Committee

Almost at once two Normies came bursting into the room. They looked to be the same ones who had been chasing Otto. After a word from the Mayor they seized the two Councillors and marched them out of the room.

Everyone else, except Elfina, looked down at the table in front of them throughout the whole thing. It was horrible.

Then Elfina cracked her knuckles slowly one after the other. A truly sickening sound.

'Fortunately,' she said, 'I have been to the Outside many times. And I remember everything perfectly. It is really not so different except, of course, there are no magicos. If you will tell me any ideas you have for things to go on the Impossible List then I will tell you if I agree. And may I say what an excellent idea this Impossible List is. And how I admire his Mayorfulness.'

'Why don't you start, Councillor Pinkbod,' invited the Mayor. Looking rather pink himself.

'What about those very small dogs,' suggested Councillor Pinkbod in a scared voice.

'How do you mean, Councillor?'

'Well some dogs like, er, wolf-hounds, they're very big aren't they? And then there's middle-sized dogs. But, er, then there's these very small ones. Yorkshire terriers and things. Well you don't get that with other animals do you? You don't get very small cows, or camels, or . . .'

'What do you think, my swee— er, Councillor Crink,' asked the Mayor, turning to Elfina.

Otto thought he saw a smile flicker in Elfina Crink's eyes. The rest of her face didn't move.

'Interesting. We will do research,' she said.

'What about the fact that it's always cold and snowy in the Winter Gardens where the ice rink is, even when it's summer everywhere else,' said somebody. 'Isn't that Impossible?'

'Absolutely not,' said Elfina sharply.

'What about the Bouncing Playground,' suggested the same voice, not to be put off, it seemed, 'with those trampolines. And the Bouncing Pavements. Is it Normal for children to go fifty feet into the air and land safely? Isn't that rather high?'

'Absolutely not,' said Elfina, 'it is perfectly Possible and Respectable.'

'Do you think the crate birds are totally Normal?' ventured somebody. 'Do they have birds on the Outside that are so big and build their nests out of scrap metal and old tram seats and so forth? And the midsummer butterflies, are all butterflies a couple of feet across? And are sheep usually so intelligent?'

'All completely Normal,' interrupted Elfina crisply. 'However, it has occurred to me that there is something you should put on your list. Cats.'

'Cats!' exclaimed several people at once, including Mayor Crumb.

'Not all cats are Impossible,' continued Elfina mysteriously, 'but some are. An Impossible cat could be in league with the magicos. Until we have an easy way of detecting which are which, we plan to arrest them all.'

'But I've got two lovely cats. I don't want anything to happen to them!' cried the woman who had been blocking her ears. She looked horrified. She wasn't the only one.

'Thank you for coming forward with that information, Councillor,' said Elfina, very smooth. 'I will send some of my Police around to your house to collect them in the morning.'

'But there's nothing wrong with my cats, really, I've had them ever since they were kittens. They're sweet, sweet, lovable—'

'Councillor,' interrupted Elfina, 'if your cats are eventually found to be innocent then they will merely be taken out of the City Gates and released. It is safer for the City to have no cats at all. We have reason to believe that there is a connection between some cats, the Impossible ones, and a particular sort of magico called a widge. The cats may be involved in making Impossible Things happen. Have any holes appeared in the road near where you live?'

There was now a tense silence in the room, disturbed only by the snivelling of the woman who was going to be visited by the Police.

Mayor Crumb picked up his pen in his big hands and then put it down.

'Perhaps, in this case, given the Councillor's excellent record of service to the City—'

'With respect, no exceptions can be made. There may be a small number of magicos living in the City itself. Their friends and neighbours may believe them to be perfectly Normal. Perhaps the Councillor herself knows more about this practice than we were aware. Perhaps she has good reason to fear a visit from my Police, who are after all highly trained to detect magicos, however Normal they may seem.'

Nobody spoke. They didn't even move.

'And little pocket mirrors,' said Elfina. 'We believe they are also used by magicos for Impossible purposes. Anyone carrying such a mirror is suspect. Remember it may not be their fault, but really the magicos are the enemies of our City. We will never prosper until they are all under control and doing sensible jobs to keep them busy.'

Mayor Crumb declared the meeting closed and the Councillors began to leave. Otto could see him patting nervously at the top pocket of his jacket, where he had put his mirror and comb after tidying his hair before Elfina arrived.

'I thought it wasn't such a good idea to start with, but I think your Impossible List may be useful after all,' said Elfina, when they were alone.

'Oh, my sweet,' said the Mayor, 'it's all for you, you know.'

'You're absolutely right,' said Elfina. 'It certainly is. By the way, I'm getting the Normal Police to move the magicos out of the mud towns.'

'But why? Where will they go?'

'I'm sure we'll find somewhere for them. If we clean up that whole stretch of the river it'll be a lovely spot. A holiday destination; I'll put up some hotels. And I'm going to build an arena. For shows and public entertainments. The magicos can do tricks for us all to watch. That seems a sensible way to employ them, don't you think? Perhaps you could get me some money from the Treasury.'

'Whatever you say, my love,' said Mayor Crumb. 'I heard that the Normal Police were down at the mud towns last night questioning a lot of magicos, is that to do with your plans to build a hotel?'

Elfina dropped her voice. 'Between you and me I'm looking for a particular magico. Every now and then one of them is born with a certain mark, a birthmark in the shape of a butterfly. It's all rubbish but one of their primitive ideas is that these people have to be, well, leaders in a way.'

She hesitated, the casual tone which she had been using had gone.

'No, not leaders exactly, there isn't really anything like it in our way of life. They call them kings or queens, but it's not

the same meaning, they have to try and help their people if they can. It's a question of honour.'

'Do they have crowns and jewels? Do they throw people into dungeons?' asked Mayor Crumb, much intrigued.

'No, no, no. It's not like that. Anyway the last few have all been useless. The thing is that the one they're supposed to have now disappeared. No one has seen him for years. He was very quiet as a kid. Bit of a scholar. Skinny.'

'You know so much about them, so many of their strange primitive ways,' said Mayor Crumb admiringly. 'It's almost as if you'd lived in the mud towns to do research.'

'Oh. Please don't insult me,' said Elfina, and Otto heard a distant note of fear in her voice. 'The next thing is you'll be saying I talk like one.'

The Mayor clasped his hands together in horror.

'My dearest pumpkins, no, no, of course not.'

'Not even when I talk about yellow fruit—'

'But of course not, my darling, you talk about yellow fruit just like any other well brought up person from The Heights.'

'Because I am from The Heights you know. *My* father was a merchant before he retired and my mother is a perfect citizen. She loves me more than anything.'

Elfina's voice had dropped almost to a whisper.

'You know, Cedric,' she added, 'my childhood was so sheltered, up on The Heights, that when my spies tell me about the mud towns, even now I can be shocked. Apparently sometimes the mothers just walk out and leave their children. They are so different from us, like animals.'

'Yes, my darling,' said the Mayor soothingly. 'And we are so refined. And you are so beautiful. Your hair is like silk.'

'Oh, so is yours, Cedric.'

'And your hands are like little graceful birds—'

'Oh, so are yours, Cedric.'

And they went out of the door, cooing to one another.

At last Otto was alone.

For a moment he stayed perfectly still.

He must get home immediately and talk to his father. He must make him listen.

Dolores would be really worried by now. It would soon be dark. Maybe she'd phone the police.

This was such a very unhappy thought that it gave him enough energy to punch miserably at the grille in front of him.

It was loose. At least one screw was moving. He pushed it and shook it. It came looser. One big shove and it crashed on to the floor below.

Otto crawled further along the shaft, came back feet first and a moment later was on the floor too.

He ran over to the nearest window, opened it and dived out into an alleyway full of dustbins.

BACK TO THE Flat

Otto thundered past Mrs Thudbutton who wrote down in her note-book, 'Otto Hush, little boy flat 15 in very late.' She was spying on everyone in the building, hoping to get a reward for finding a magico family.

He pressed the button for the lift, couldn't bear to wait and started to run up the stairs. His legs seemed to be screaming. His throat was on fire.

At last he reached the front door.

Dolores opened it.

'Where's Dad?'

'He's working all night at the library, where on earth have you been?'

'WORKING ALL NIGHT?'

She slammed the door behind him and snapped the bolts across.

'I've got to see him, it's really important.'

'Where have you been, Ottie? It's dark nearly. I told you not to stay out in the dark. You only went for some porridge bowls. I nearly phoned the police.'

Granny Culpepper came out of the twins' room. She was splattered with something. She looked like a statue that birds like sitting on. Hepzie and Zeb bobbed in the air over her head, neither were wearing nappies.

'Ottie! Ottie!' they cried happily and shot towards him. Zeb kicking Granny Culpepper on the nose as they went past.

'Dad never works all night.'

'Well he is now, Otto, there must be something very important he has to do.'

Granny Culpepper snorted.

'But, Mum, I saw this meeting in the Town Hall, all about Impossible Things and that woman was there, from the telly and Mayor Crumb, and she says no one should have a cat and she's looking for someone with a certain birthmark and it sounded just like the one Dad has that he used to hide with a sticking plaster when we went swimming. And I think it's him. I think he's the King of the Karmidee.'

No one spoke.

Then, 'The King of the Karmidee,' whispered Dolores softly. 'Do they have kings? I never heard of that . . .'

'That has nothing to do with your father,' interrupted Granny Culpepper, even more firmly than usual. 'Albert a Karmidee indeed! He is a Respectable person. Useless but Respectable.'

'Oh, Mother,' said Dolores wearily.

The twins had floated off to the bathroom and Otto moved to follow.

'Well it's true that he's useless,' he heard Granny Culpepper continue in a lower voice, 'telling you all those lies and now hiding away in that library. Is he descended from bandits, or outlaws or time travellers or magicians or alchemists or dragon charmers or what, may I ask? Sugar mice by the look of him, like the ones on those toys.'

She meant the mobiles.

'Oh, Mother,' said Dolores.

'Ottie bubble, Ottie bubble,' sang the twins hopefully.

'Come out of there, Otto,' called Granny Culpepper, 'I will deal with this. One must be firm. It is past their bedtime.'

For a few minutes afterwards Otto and Dolores stayed in the corridor by the front door listening to Granny Culpepper informing the twins that they must come down at once.

Then there was a terrible crash. She had climbed on to the

basin to try and catch them. The whole thing had come off the wall.

Unhurt but enraged beyond endurance Granny Culpepper remained on the floor for some time.

'I am Respectable!' she yelled, 'YOU are Respectable, HE is Respectable, WE are Respectable, THEY are just dancing.'

'Oh, Mother,' said Dolores.

Afterwards Otto lay in bed, listening to Dolores singing lullabies to the twins. She used to sing like that to him, long ago. Of course he wouldn't like her to do it now because he was too grown-up.

The dragons and spiders hung very still. No breeze tonight. He almost hated the mobiles now. It had been really good designing them and making them with Albert but Granny Culpepper was right, they were just toys. The world was full of secrets and dangers and his father hadn't come home. Maybe this was just the beginning. Maybe he would never come home again. Maybe he really was hiding in the library. Hiding in the books.

He was almost asleep, because he was very very tired, when he suddenly thought of Mab. If anyone else needed to know about the meeting and everything he'd heard, it was her. As soon as the flat had gone quiet he got up and dressed again.

Then he crept out of the front door, up the back stairs to the top floor, through a small door marked 'Garden' and then up some more stairs on to the roof.

Like many buildings in the City, Hershell Buildings had a roof garden. There were even trees.

Not only that, the roof gardens led into one another. Some were joined by rope bridges suspended high above the streets.

Otto jogged from garden to garden, past ponds and pergolas and picnic tables until he was at the furthest end of Parry Street. Well away from the flat in case the worst happened and the same Normies came and spotted him again.

He opened the box where he kept the beetle and peered inside. The beetle seemed to be resting.

Feeling foolish, he whispered, 'Go and get Mab.'

To his surprise it started to shuffle around. Then it opened its emerald carapace, took off briefly and sat down again with a thud.

Otto waited anxiously.

Perhaps it was thinking.

Or perhaps it was just a normal beetle that Mab had given him. A shiny green joke indeed.

Then he jerked his head back just in time as it rose vertically and Impossibly with a deep buzzing noise and lumbered through the air, turning sharp right over the lime trees.

Otto lost sight of it. The buzzing grew fainter in the distance.

Some people went past on the pavement below. Then a two-seater penny-farthing bicycle, the big wheel glowing with a spiral of coloured lightbulbs. A woman's voice saying, '. . . did you see that street-cleaning machine, wasn't there something on the back?'

'Not our problem,' said the man. 'They're just doing their job.'

'Look out!' There was a crunch. The penny-farthings, which were for hire, were famous for falling over.

'I thought this was supposed to be romantic,' said the woman, sitting on the pavement.

There was a hissing sound from further down the street. Otto held tightly to the empty box. Maybe it was just a real street-cleaning machine, they were up and down Parry Street most nights.

Then he saw it and stifled a scream. It was a Normal Police one all right, the same Normies too.

The people on the penny-farthing had just sorted themselves out.

There was a cage on the back of the cleaning machine with a child in it, crying and holding on to the bars.

They ignored it all and pedalled off.

And now with the machine directly below and shining its

searchlight all around, *now* Mab came swooping down.

She saw the Normies just before they saw her.

The carpet hovered.

Otto, terrified, waved at her to go.

He glimpsed the beetle glittering like a brooch on her shoulder.

'You're evil!' she yelled at him. 'You've called me so that they can catch me!'

'No!' screamed Otto above the terrible hiss of the machine.

The child in the cage was frantically rattling the bars and calling something to Mab. Otto couldn't make it out.

'I hate you!' shouted Mab.

'No! I'm one of them! I'm one of you!' cried Otto. 'My father isn't really called Hush! My father's real name is Karmidee, I'm sure of it—'

'Oh please,' she sneered.

The carpet dropped down to the back of the machine and the Normie fired his terrible net for the first time. The searchlight scanned the air, resting on Otto. He picked up a garden table.

Mab had climbed right onto the back of the machine. She was struggling to open the cage.

One of the Normies was pulling himself towards her along the top.

Otto, groaning with effort, threw the table off the roof. It missed the Normie and splintered uselessly on the road. Some lights came on in the buildings opposite.

Mab was pulling the child through the cage door. The carpet hovered bobbing beside her. Both the Normies were shouting. The nearer one reached out. Mab and the little girl from the cage were trapped, clinging to the truck. The Normie was between them and the carpet.

Then suddenly he wasn't.

He was lying in the road. He'd been hit on the leg by a plant pot.

The carpet, with its two passengers, rose up to the roof.

The net thudded against the side of the building, spread out in the air and settled on the top of the nearest tree.

'It's not how it looks—' cried Otto.

'What do you mean you're one of us?' Mab interrupted, haughty and white-faced. The little girl huddled behind her, all eyes.

'Just go!' cried Otto.

'So are you or aren't you, little boy?'

'My father, it's not his real name, he changed it, I think he's called Albert Karmidee . . . maybe not even Albert, maybe he changed that too.'

The Normal Police were struggling with their net. Windows were opening along Parry Street.

'Your father,' she said, full of contempt, 'Albert Karmidee . . . no, I don't think so.'

She stayed a moment longer, giving him a merciless stare with the blue-white lamps of her eyes. Then the carpet lifted away. Up into the sultry night.

Otto AT THE Library

It was the following morning.

Albert Hush had left for work before any of his family woke up and had at last finished copying the Karmidee document in secret.

Now he and the Junior Assistant Under Librarian, Miss Fringe, were peering into the Reading Room from a hole in an oil painting. Unknown to the public the library was full of secret doors, passages and spy holes.

'That's her, Mr Hush,' whispered Miss Fringe, 'she's been looking through all the ancient manuscripts since this morning. Town Hall ID and two Normies with her. She's only looking at the Karmidee stuff. I'm afraid she even made me get the really delicate papers out

of the temperature-controlled cases. Says she's looking for a particular document. Thinks we may have it here. Asked for the Karmidee expert. I said you were at lunch.'

'Did she say anything else?'

'No. But you know who it is, it's that Elfina Crink, Mr Hush. I've seen her on telly.'

'So have I,' said Albert softly.

Then he saw something else and groaned. 'Oh no, Otto, not now. Miss Fringe, my son has just come into the Reading Room and is for some reason hiding behind a pillar. Go and fetch him and bring him here please.'

Miss Fringe hesitated. She was being tugged about by the Rules of the Library on one side and her loyalty to Mr Hush on the other.

'But Mr Hush, only Staff are supposed—'

'JUST DO IT PLEASE, I will take responsibility.'

Otto couldn't see his father anywhere. He could see the woman in the raincoat and the two Normies. The same ones who he kept seeing everywhere. What were they doing here? Now he was stuck in the corner behind this stupid pillar and any moment they might see him again.

Suddenly a door opened in the shelves beside him, a door made of shelves it seemed, and someone reached out, grabbed him and pulled him inside.

'Please come this way,' said Miss Fringe, breaking Library Rule 39.

They hurried along wooden passages, past mysterious doors and little twisted staircases and came quickly upon Albert, still by the spy hole.

'I hope you've got a very good reason for coming here,' he said to Otto.

Otto wanted to hit him.

'No one will listen to me. I was in the Town Hall heating system. I saw a meeting . . .'

Otto stopped. He'd suddenly realized that Miss Fringe was standing there and could hear everything.

He pulled a face, trying to signal to his father. But Albert had life and death on his mind and kept looking through the spy hole.

'What do you mean you were in the heating system? Is that what you came to tell me?'

'I saw a meeting . . .' mumbled Otto, '. . . that woman was there. The one in the big room now, wearing the raincoat, she's got these two Normies with her, she's the one I saw and she hates magicos, Dad, she said . . .'

'Miss Fringe,' interrupted Albert suddenly, 'please don't take any notice of my son, he lives in a fantasy world. You must have plenty to do. I'm going to my desk now. Just come and fetch me when you need me.'

Miss Fringe, helpful as ever, walked quickly and quietly out of earshot.

'Dad,' began Otto, desperately.

'Be quiet please,' said Albert in a voice full of something.

Otto's eyes were beginning to heat up.

Albert grabbed his wrist and hurried him off down the passage and then through a door into a proper room again with windows and desks. The Staff Offices. No one else was there.

'Right, now,' said Albert, breathing carefully, 'I'm going to give you something which you must hide in your clothes. Take it out of the library. Take it home. KEEP IT IN YOUR CLOTHES. Don't take it out even to sleep. They may search the flat. Now. That woman out there. Tell me what you saw when you were in the radiator.'

'Oh, Dad,' said Otto, tears on his face, 'I wasn't in the radiator, I was running away from some Normies in Banzee, Smith and Banzee . . .'

'Just tell me what you saw.'

'She's the new Minister for Modernization. The Mayor calls her sweetheart and angel. She's going to put hotels where the mud towns are and she says cats and dogs and little mirrors are Impossible and magicos are enemies. And she has to find a magico with a certain mark. The Karmidee King.'

Albert was pulling drawers open, looking for things.

'I knew it,' he muttered. 'Look, Otto, it's time for me to go. I've got something important to work out. Something to solve, like a riddle. It's what I have to do, do you understand? For my people. She's been looking for me already, in the mud towns. If she sees me now she'll recognize me. We knew each other a long time ago.'

He pulled an envelope out of some sort of hidden compartment and pushed it down the front of Otto's shirt.

'Dad . . .'

Albert opened the nearest window, got a whistle out of his pocket and blew it. There was a tiny sound.

'It's very high-pitched,' he said, as if that explained everything.

His face was grey.

'Tell your mum what I've told you and wait for a message from me. We are all in danger.'

Albert stopped talking and doing things.

'Dad, you are a Karmidee, aren't you,' whispered Otto.

Albert didn't reply.

'DAD JUST TELL ME. Mum knows, doesn't she?'

'Yes, I am a Karmidee, I'm . . .'

The room was beginning to fill with light. Red, orange, lemon, green, gorgeous, like being inside a jewel. Then finally a turquoise. As if they stood on the bottom of a tropical sea.

At this extraordinary moment Miss Fringe walked in.

Albert was shaking. He dropped some papers he was holding.

Otto saw Miss Fringe reach out her hand. He saw the papers flutter one by one up to her fingers.

Albert stared at her.

'Dad?' whispered Otto.

'It's all right,' said Albert, taking his hand.

And for a moment it was. The warm sea colours ran down the walls and withdrew across the carpet, until just a glowing pool was left where Albert and Otto stood together.

Miss Fringe held out the papers Albert had dropped.

Then the door burst open. Not the door to the maze of passages, the real door from the Reading Room on which, in gold letters, it said LIBRARIANS ONLY.

The sign had not deterred Elfina. She marched in now, followed by her two Normies and a nervous but determined member of the library staff.

'Mr Hush will join you in the Reading Room directly. If you would be so kind as to wait at your table—'

'I've been waiting ten minutes,' said Elfina. 'I don't expect to wait at all. Where is this expert? I want—'

She stopped. She'd seen Albert.

'This is Mr Hush,' said the Senior Shelf Duster. 'Now if you would just return—'

'This is Mr Hush, is it?' said Elfina more quietly. 'Well, I never did.'

Miss Fringe stepped in front of Otto, as if she could shield him.

Elfina stared and stared at Albert.

'Mr Hush,' she said at last, in a softer voice, 'what a quiet name you have. Like a whisper. Almost invisible.'

He inclined his head as if acknowledging a compliment.

'I've looked for you in so many places,' she continued. 'I never thought of this one, right here in the library on the Boulevard.'

'We have both come a long way,' said Albert courteously.

There was a silence between them as if no one else was there.

'I came to see a certain document,' said Elfina at last. 'I've been looking for it just as I've been looking for you. I expected it to be rotting away in some hiding place somewhere in the mud towns but I underestimated you. It's here.'

She put a piece of parchment on the table. The one Albert had been copying in secret.

'Perhaps if you would return to the Reading Room—' repeated the Senior Shelf Duster.

'It's all right,' said Albert, dismissing him, 'we'll look at this in here. Please go and see if anyone needs any help.'

He went over to a table near the window and sat down.

Elfina followed him, gesturing to the Normies who waited by the door. They hadn't noticed Otto properly yet.

'This is a very early document,' began Albert, 'extremely fragile. That is why it is kept in our temperature-controlled section. Humidity is also a problem.'

'Go on.'

'It was recovered from the roots of a tree by the river many years ago and donated to the library for safe-keeping. Kept in a normal atmosphere, it would, unfortunately, deteriorate rapidly.'

'Go on.'

'It appears to tell a story of something which might happen. A story of different possibilities. Some Karmidee were troubled by visions of this kind and it was their custom to write or draw what they could remember as best they could, and bury it. Preferably near a tree.'

'And?'

'A woman is shown here standing on a pile of coins. She appears to be holding the City in her hands. See her?'

They were both looking down at the parchment and to Otto, watching, it seemed almost as if they were friends and Albert was trying to warn her of something, as a friend will warn a friend. Even when they are sure they won't be heard.

'She must deny herself,' he said softly, 'and what will happen if we deny ourselves? If we forget the beginning? If the enemy we despise is really in our hearts?'

She looked at him and the armour of her face began to change.

'There's that kid!' shouted one of the Normies.

Elfina's face locked shut again.

'Down!' she commanded. 'Sit!'

'The one who looks out of windows and throws things off the roof and nearly killed me with a plant pot, the one who got away on the Boulevard using some sort of magico trick, some degenerate, crazy, magico—'

'ALL RIGHT!' she said. 'Arrest him and shut up. I need to know the end of this story.'

The Normies stood up again.

'What has he done?' asked Albert, also standing.

'He's a magico!' chorused the Normies.

'Don't touch him!' cried Miss Fringe.

'HE IS MY SON,' said Albert.

The Normies both lunged at Otto and were briefly entangled with Miss Fringe.

Albert leapt up, flung open the door into the little passage and shoved Otto through in front of him.

Otto heard it thud shut. He turned to Albert behind him but Albert wasn't behind him. He was alone. He rattled at the

little door. It wouldn't open. On the other side he heard Elfina saying, 'Don't move, Al.'

Colour started to pour through the cracks around the door.

'Dad!' screamed Otto.

'Don't let him get away!' from Elfina.

An unbelievable sound, like a huge tent flapping in a storm, crashing, glass breaking. Normies shouting.

Otto pulled and wrenched at the door. But it was locked. And he was left there sobbing and struggling as wave after wave of colour flooded into the passage. Bitter yellow. Red like blood.

Then the noise on the other side had stopped.

Whatever had happened had finished. Otto felt the door handle turn as if it unlocked itself. He stepped back into his father's office.

No one was there. Desks and furniture lay scattered. Something very big had happened to the window. The top part had been open already, of course, but it obviously hadn't been big enough and now the bottom was smashed. The little glass panes, and the bands of wood that had held them, had splintered.

'Dad?' whispered Otto.

He walked a little further into the room and felt something creak inside his shirt. The envelope. The one he must not take out, in case they searched the flat.

A terrifying picture flashed into his head.

The Normies dragging away his mother and the twins. Maybe at this very moment.

He heard voices on the other side of the door that led into the Reading Room. It was slightly open.

'. . . coming from in there,' said somebody. 'Sounded like glass to me.'

'I saw them come out,' said someone else. 'They all went back to the Main Entrance I think. It didn't look good.'

Otto looked round. He didn't know the way out through the mysterious passages. The window looked much too dangerous. Then he saw a door in the corner marked Fire Exit.

He was closing it softly behind him as the Senior Shelf Duster and a number of concerned citizens came in through 'Librarians Only'.

Never had it seemed to take so long to get home from anywhere before.

GRANNY Culpepper AND Shinnabac

Everybody was in the kitchen.

'The Normies came to the library with that woman,' gasped Otto, hardly able to speak, leaning on the door.

'You've been running—'

'Yes, yes, Mum, I think they've got Dad. Or maybe he escaped but I think they might come here. Now, they might come NOW.'

'Got your dad? What do you mean?'

'The twins, Dolores,' said Granny Culpepper quickly. 'Get them down, they mustn't dance so high, it doesn't look respectable.'

Hepzie and Zeb were standing upside down with their feet on the ceiling. It was a new game.

There was a thunderous knocking on the door.

'Open up!' shouted a man's voice. 'Normal Police! Impossible Enquiries!'

Everyone froze, wide-eyed.

'Shinnabac!' called Granny Culpepper, taking off her apron.

Otto jumped on the table to try and reach the twins.

'We'll deal with this, Dolores,' said Granny Culpepper, not specifying who 'we' were going to be. 'Let them in and try to keep them away from this room as long as you can.'

'But, Mother, how—'

'Hurry!'

Shinnabac wandered sleepily in from the living room and Granny Culpepper closed the kitchen door behind him. The twins floated down to give Otto a hug.

'We have reason to believe that this is the residence of Albert Hush, magico, guilty of Impossible Activities,' said a voice at the front door, all too familiar to Otto.

'They know me, it's them, they'll recognize me,' he said desperately. He couldn't see how Granny Culpepper was going to be able to do anything.

'Give the twins to me. Get in the cupboard under the sink,' she commanded.

He squeezed in among washing-up liquid and soap powder and she closed the door behind him. There was a crack along the top big enough to see through.

This was insane, the twins would wriggle, they always wriggled. Any minute now they'd fly.

Shinnabac started behaving very strangely. He climbed quickly onto the table and sat there very upright.

Then Granny Culpepper let go of the struggling twins.

How could he have been so stupid! Of course, she despised Albert, she was going to betray them all!

'No!' he screamed.

'Don't move!' she hissed back.

The twins made for his little door, started kicking it. 'Ottie! Ottie!'

'Calm, Otto!' whispered Granny Culpepper, all intensity, staring at Shinnabac and holding her head up with every bit of her energy coming out of her eyes.

She lifted her arm and pointed at her cat, and Shinnabac, suddenly gorgeous and dangerous, fixed his stare on the twins.

In the background Otto could hear the Normies talking to Dolores as they came out of the living room.

'They're coming . . .' he groaned, in agony.

The twins' long frizzy hair stood out as if it was electrified and, giggling, they began to sail upwards and backwards while Granny Culpepper and Shinnabac stared. They landed gently on the table, side by side.

'Is this the kitchen?' asked a voice outside.

Still Granny Culpepper didn't move.

The twins curled up on the table and they snuggled down as if it was the softest bed in the world. They had fallen asleep.

Granny Culpepper and Shinnabac relaxed at last and Otto watched with his mouth open as she picked a blanket out of the laundry basket and tucked it lovingly over his sisters.

The kitchen door opened and Mr Eight came in with Dolores behind him with her hands clasped in terror.

'Good morning,' said Granny Culpepper, in her Heights accent, 'how can I help you? We were just about to have some lemon tea and lemon cake with lemon filling and lemon icing.'

Dolores had spotted the twins and her eyes were like saucers.

'I must search the room,' said Mr Eight.

'Is there a problem?' asked Granny Culpepper sweetly.

'I'm afraid there is, we are searching this residence for Suspicious and Impossible Items of a Non-Respectable Nature.'

Mr Eight was opening cupboard doors, working his way towards the sink. Dolores peered around for Otto.

Granny Culpepper stepped nearer to his hiding place with a cosy, motherly sort of smile.

'Oh my, this one's locked,' she said. 'Dolores dear, fetch the key.'

'The key,' repeated Dolores. After all there was no keyhole.

'Yes, dear, fetch it would you, it's in the drawer isn't it?'

Shinnabac had sidled up to Mr Eight.

'The key,' Dolores muttered, starting to open drawers. Otto could see her hands shaking.

Shinnabac stared at Mr Eight and Granny Culpepper stared at Shinnabac.

Mr Eight had his face right up to the crack above the door and he was reaching for the handle. Otto, crammed against the other side, watched in awe. Mr Eight was having some sort of change of mood. A different expression, almost pleasant, spread across his unlovely features. He stood up.

'We'll leave that one,' he said. 'What darling little babies, aren't they sweet.'

'Aren't they?' enthused Granny Culpepper.

'I was a baby once, you know,' said Mr Eight.

'Really, dear, how nice.'

'And what a beautiful cat as well.'

'We like to think so. Dolores, do put the kettle on.' Granny Culpepper picked Shinnabac up and put him in the laundry basket, just as Mr Six came in.

'Can't find much—'

'All done in here,' interrupted Mr Eight cheerfully. 'We're going to have a cup of tea.'

'Should we have tea on duty?' said Mr Six, doubtfully.

'All right, we'll go to the park instead!' cried Mr Eight,

seizing the stunned Mr Six by the hand. 'It's a wonderful world!'

'Weren't we supposed to arrest—'

'Race you to the swings!' chimed Mr Eight. He skipped out of the flat, dragging Mr Six behind him.

Immediately the twins began to wake up. Granny Culpepper gave Shinnabac two tins of sardines while Otto and Dolores, wild-eyed, watched her without speaking.

'Are you all right, Mother?' whispered Dolores eventually.

'I am a little tired, dear, and I have to write a letter. I think it would be best if I could be by myself.'

They took the twins into the living room and, after a while, Otto recounted everything that had happened at the library.

'You're telling me he IS some sort of king or something?' said Dolores. 'And he knew Elfina before, a long time ago?'

'He has to do what he can for his people, it's a matter of honour.'

'Albert? A matter of honour? He makes mobiles and works in a library.'

THE Unicorn

About half an hour later there was a peculiar noise.

'Mother?' called Dolores, running along the corridor.

There was a unicorn in the kitchen. Rust-coloured.

'Granny's disappeared,' explained Dolores, 'and this unicorn is here.'

'Ganny! Ganny!' sang Hepzie, pointing at the unicorn.

'Granny was here,' said Dolores slowly. 'Now this unicorn is here instead.'

The letter which Granny Culpepper had been writing was on the kitchen table.

My dear Dolores,

I'm afraid this is going to come as a bit of a shock

to you. Daddy and I didn't want you ever to know but the way things have turned out it does seem that you have to.

The truth is, my dear, that although my parents had that little shop near Guido's Beach that I've told you about, my father's mother came from TigerHouse and I am a widge.

Dolores was reading this out loud to Otto.

'Do you know what a widge is?' she asked him.

'A sort of Karmidee, Mum, they make magic spells using cats I think.' He glanced over at Shinnabac who was taking the opportunity to lick out the butter dish.

I hadn't used my powers for many years. I wanted to live a Normal Life with your daddy and give you a Respectable Childhood.

When the Normal Police came for Albert I had to put a spell on the girls to stop them flying. Shinnabac amplified for me. You know they would have taken them away.

The trouble is that if widges use their powers for the first time in a long time, especially at my age, it can have a very tiring effect.

So very tiring, in fact, that it may be necessary for them to become a unicorn for a while. We are

closely related I think, I've never understood it all myself. Being a unicorn takes a little less cosmic energy.

My dear. I have been Normal and Respectable for so long but in truth it has been a terrible strain and very tiring and I HAVE OFTEN HAD A HEADACHE. Now that I've allowed myself to use my powers again I feel really rather jolly.

Really, it was wrong not to educate you properly in your heritage. Daddy wouldn't have minded as long as they didn't find out at the Town Hall and the Golf Club.

I think I'm beginning to feel a horn starting to come out of my forehead. I hope it's a pretty spirally one . . .

The pen skidded a bit along the page after that and there was no more writing. Difficult, presumably, to hold a pen in your hoof.

A silence fell in No 15 Hershell Buildings, broken only by the rather heavy breathing of the unicorn.

'She's one of them,' whispered Dolores, her voice faint with shock. 'I'm the daughter of a magico, I'm—'

'Ganny!' cried Hepzie. She floated over and sat on the unicorn's back.

'Well it *is* a spirally horn,' said Dolores, as her eyes filled with tears.

'Perhaps she'd like a mirror,' said Otto.

'When I've had a coffee,' said Dolores.

The unicorn had some coffee too. And a lettuce.

Then they heard a knock at the door.

THE isitor

It was Mrs Thudbutton looking puffed-up, nasty and pleased with herself, and a very strange-looking person in a big hat with wax cherries on it.

'You've got a visitor, Mrs Hush,' said Mrs Thudbutton, 'and there's this letter for your son, I thought I'd bring it up.'

The visit from the Normal Police had confirmed her suspicion that the family in No 15 weren't Normal. She was full of contempt for them and furious that she hadn't got a reward.

'Please come in,' said Dolores to the person in the hat.

'NO, sorry,' said Mrs Thudbutton. 'Normal Police said no visitors up here. I've only let her come up as a favour.'

It wasn't a favour, of course, it was because she thought she'd find out something more and maybe get a reward after all.

Otto stood next to his mother.

No one spoke. They were all waiting for Mrs Thudbutton to go. Except she didn't. She handed an envelope to Otto. He could see that it had already been opened.

The person with the big hat coughed.

'Get on with it,' said Mrs Thudbutton, enjoying herself.

Otto, being small, could see the visitor's face better than anyone else. Despite the fact that it was smeared with make-up and almost completely hidden behind enormous dark glasses, he felt sure he'd seen it somewhere before.

'Just a social visit, Dolores,' said a voice from under the hat.

'Of course,' said Dolores, 'lovely to see you. I'm sorry I'm not properly dressed.'

'Get on with it,' said Mrs Thudbutton gleefully.

The person with the big hat clearly had something important to say and couldn't say it because of Mrs Thudbutton.

A neighing sound came from the kitchen and both Dolores and Otto started coughing extravagantly to try and cover it up. Otto did such a good pretend cough that he started coughing properly. Any minute now the twins would come floating through.

'Otto,' said the visitor in a rush, 'do you remember the woman with the big, er, dog? The one that likes liquorice?'

Otto didn't. He nodded.

'Well, it's her birthday. It's her birthday today. I thought you might have forgotten. Come along tonight. To her place. She's so respectable. We're all going to be there. We'll sing a few of the wonderful songs in the new *Glad to Be Normal Songbook*. Just bring some liquorice.'

The visitor reached out and touched Dolores' arm. 'All of you,' she added. 'The whole family.'

'Thank you,' said Dolores. 'We'd love to.'

'But—' began Otto.

'It's such a big dog, isn't it, Otto,' gushed the visitor chattily, 'such a very very big dog. A VERY BIG ONE.'

Mrs Thudbutton's telephone echoed up from her concierge's office in the entrance hall.

'That'll do,' snapped Mrs Thudbutton, who now rather fancied herself as a policewoman or a prison warder in the movies.

'I don't think these people will be going anywhere. Mr Hush has been arrested. I have been told to contact the Normal Police if any member of his family tries to leave the building.'

'Mrs Thudbutton,' said Dolores, drawing herself up to her tallest, 'my husband is a respectable citizen. If he has been arrested then it is a mistake and he will be released very soon.'

There was a gentle thump of hooves on the carpet behind her. She nodded a polite goodbye to the visitor.

'So sorry, I have to go now, I was just going to, er, to have a bath.'

'May you wash your cares away,' whispered the visitor in return.

Dolores shut the door in a hurry, just as the unicorn arrived, accompanied by spinning twins and a fine rain of scrambled eggs.

'Did you know that woman, Otto? Do you know what she meant?'

'I know I've seen her somewhere, Mum.' He jumbled the clues around in his head. Dog, liquorice, dog, liquorice, dog, liquorice, dog . . .

'She was in some sort of disguise, wasn't she? Not a very good one either. Put that down, Zebbie! Did you see her hand? It was a different colour from her face.' Dolores puzzled over this. 'She must have put something on her face and forgotten to put it on her hand, or not had time or something. Maybe there's something very distinctive about her face, Ottie. And she knew all our names. Do you think your father could have sent her? Do you think it's a message from him?'

'Wash your cares away!' cried Otto. 'Today and every day! It's the launderette. The FireBox. I went there with Dad and he went round into a back room. There was a dragon there, Mum, a real one. It picked him up by the leg and it ate liquorice! Not a dog, a dragon, not a dog, a—'

'A dragon? At the launderette? By the leg?'

'Yes, and that's where we're supposed to go.'

'But this woman at the door. It might all be a trap.'

Otto clapped his hands on each side of his head.

'It's her! It's Miss Fridge!'

'From the library?'

'Yes, she's like me, lots of freckles. Except hers are sort of reddish. And they make a pattern on the side of her face, here. It's like a sort of heart shape. That's what she was trying to hide because it's very, you know, Mrs Thudbutton would notice that for sure. Didn't you see her hand? All freckles. She helped Dad, yesterday, or tried to . . .'

He found the sentence too difficult and stopped.

'From the library?' repeated Dolores.

'She works there. She's the one I told you about. In the little passages. She was brave.' He paused again. 'So was Dad.'

They looked at each other.

'We've got to get out of here. We've got to go to the launderette,' said Dolores. 'It's not a party.'

Hepzie swooped down and kissed Otto on the nose. She smelt of toast.

They bolted the door and began to look for things to pack.

Otto finally looked at his letter. It was crumpled but clear enough. He ripped at the envelope, even though it had been opened already. At last, news from Dante.

> Shoes,
> Word is your dad has been arrested and you are all magicos. Can't give you my new address. Sorry. My dad has got sick. He says they're all in it. That's what it says on the telly. We had good times.
> Dante.

Otto, with a twin sitting on his head, went to his room and took down his spiders and dragons mobile. In the middle of doing it he stopped and stood at the window (shut of course) and thought of Mab and his father and everything else.

'Ottie cry. Ottie cry,' sang Hepzie sadly.

'We've got to cut your hair,' said Dolores, behind him at the bedroom door.

'What? NO, Mum. No way.'

'Yes indeed. That woman, the two Normies who keep seeing you everywhere. And now we've got to get across to HighNoon. Without your hair you'll look completely different.'

'WITHOUT my hair. How much are you going to cut off?'

Dolores was holding a pair of nail scissors in one hand and a razor of Albert's in the other.

'Is that from Dante?'

Otto shrugged. His throat felt tight.

The twins were bouncing on his bed, going right up to the ceiling. Doing back flips and somersaults.

'You two are incredible,' said Dolores.

'Impossible,' said Otto.

And they both giggled and it felt a bit like crying again.

She cut off hunks of white springy hair.

Then she began to shave it.

Then suddenly she stopped. The clock in the kitchen was striking eleven.

He had a strip of soft stubble left going over the top of his head.

'Have you finished?' he asked.

'Yes.'

'What about this bit?'

'No time. And I can hear Granny pacing about. The sooner we get her out of here the better.'

The Visitor

They hadn't dared to talk about how they would get out at all. Two flying twins. A unicorn. And Mrs Thudbutton by the doors with orders to phone the Normal Police.

THE Dragon IN THE PAVEMENT

Fortunately Mrs Thudbutton had been lazy for many years. She had allowed her mind to chug around in smaller and smaller circles as she sat down there in her little kiosk. Her new role as informer and jailor had sent her into a frenzy of self-importance and general nastiness but it hadn't given her a new brain.

'Is that Cordelia Thudbutton?' asked Dolores, trying to make her voice higher to disguise it and squeaking a bit by mistake.

'Who's this?' asked Mrs Thudbutton suspiciously.

'This is the Council, Mrs Thudbutton, I'm sorry to trouble you at such a late hour, it's the Impossible Department here. We need your help.'

There was a pause while Mrs Thudbutton tried to make sense of this information. Dolores rushed on, she was using the public telephone on the landing outside the flat, and she wasn't sure if Mrs Thudbutton might have some way of finding this out.

'We were given your name by the Citizenship Inspectors, we understand you have been put forward for a Secret Sneaky Snitch Citizen Award. The Normal Police are especially pleased with your work.'

Downstairs, Mrs Thudbutton swelled up with satisfaction. It was, she felt, no more than she deserved.

'We understand you are a person of Extreme Respectability. You are very, very Normal. An example to us all. A Role Model. The Mayor knows he can count on your loyalty. That's why we're asking for your help with a Special Mission—'

'Mitten?' It was a crackling line, as usual.

'MISSION. A Special one.' Dolores wiped some sweat off her face. She had left Otto trying to keep the twins quiet with some mashed banana.

'Have you got a pen?' she asked.

'Yes, Roger over to you, Roger,' said Mrs Thudbutton in a voice which she imagined sounded brisk and professional.

'If you leave your building, turn left and proceed along Parry Street in a westerly direction for about one quarter of a

mile you will see a manhole cover in the middle of the road.'

Dolores remembered this manhole because she had once caught the heel of her shoe in it.

Mrs Thudbutton scribbled briskly.

Otto opened the front door to see how things were going and Zeborah floated out. He made a silent grab for her but it was too late. She sat on Dolores' shoulder flicking bits of banana into her hair.

'Whatever have you got in your office?' exclaimed Mrs Thudbutton chattily. 'It sounds almost like a baby.'

'Must be a crossed line,' squeaked Dolores. 'Now, we believe that something Impossible is hiding under this manhole cover. We need you to sit on it.'

'To what on it?'

'To SIT on it. The manhole cover. Hold it down. Some Normal Police will come along soon. Usually of course we'd ask someone with Special Training but we're short staffed and your Exceptional Qualities—'

'In the middle of the road?'

'It's not in the way of the tram, citizen. But if you're scared—'

'No, no, er, what sort of Impossible Thing would it be, just out of interest?'

'We think it is a dragon. In fact you may see some smoke.'

Silence from the other end. Mrs Thudbutton's mouth was open but no sound would come out.

'Not a very big one,' gasped Dolores hoarsely, 'but nevertheless fire-breathing and quite Impossible. The important thing is to stay on the manhole cover. That way you will be absolutely safe and the Mayor will be so grateful who knows what he'll do? A reward. A medal . . . All you have to do is stay on the manhole. If anyone asks you what you're doing just explain about our phone call. Tell them you're on Official Impossible Business.'

'Roger, I'll do it,' said Mrs Thudbutton.

'We hoped you'd say that, Roger,' said Dolores.

Nathaniel Crane

A few minutes later Otto, Dolores, Granny Culpepper and the twins and Shinnabac the cat all left Hershell Buildings past the concierge's office, now empty.

They turned right and proceeded in an easterly direction.

Granny Culpepper wore a straw hat and a blanket in the hope that people would think she was a donkey. Shinnabac sat on her back, hanging on to the blanket with his claws and looking cross. The twins, in their buggy, were singing happily. Otto and Dolores were laden with bags.

It was almost midnight. They had to walk to the Boulevard, cross it and on into HighNoon.

Dolores stared up the familiar street, now full of danger.

'Look, Toes,' she said, and she hadn't called him that since he was tiny, 'if the Police come, you must try to get away with the twins. If we get split up try to get to the FireBox and don't lose that envelope Daddy gave you.'

Of course he wasn't going to lose it.

'I don't think he was arrested. I think he got away somehow,' he said, plodding fiercely along.

'Well, I hope so too,' said Dolores, not sounding as if she thought it was very likely. 'Of course I hope he wasn't arrested, but if he was then we will have to show whatever is in the envelope to somebody else. Your father, bless him, isn't a natural leader, Otto. I know he's supposed to be their King and everything—'

'He is OUR King,' yelled Otto, 'and he is WORKING on a PLAN.'

They hadn't noticed a man walking towards them and Granny Culpepper, whose hat had slipped forward over her eyes, nearly marched straight into him.

He jumped neatly out of the way. It was the thin, shabby man from the Boulevard who had nearly been taken away by the Normies that day.

'I'm terribly sorry,' said Dolores, anxiously adjusting her mother's hat. 'Are you hurt?'

'Are you crazy?' said the man.

'No, no, I do beg your pardon, my mother, um uni—

donkey couldn't see where she was going.'

'No, I mean are you crazy walking around after the curfew with a unicorn with a hat on and a large conspicuous cat? Who do you think is going to be fooled by all this? The Normies are stupid but they're not that stupid.'

Dolores stared at him.

'Plus this kid. They'll recognize him. He was nearly picked up under the tower the other day but Madame Nicely herself intervened. As you no doubt know.'

Dolores stared a bit more.

'Wakey, wakey,' said the man.

'It's the man I told you about, Mum, when that woman did something with her mirror,' said Otto.

Granny Culpepper snorted.

'I don't believe we've been introduced,' said Dolores rather haughtily.

The man laughed.

'What do you know about citrus fruit? You must be the first magico I've met who talks like The Heights.'

'I was born there,' she said simply.

He looked at her, at Otto, at them all, then behind and beyond them.

'The Normies,' he said, 'coming this way. Get the kid out of sight. Get everything out of sight.'

Dolores pushed the buggy swiftly towards an alleyway and

steered it into the dark, away from the street lamps. Everyone else followed her.

They huddled together behind some dustbins. Even Granny Culpepper sat down.

Otto saw the Normies stop at the top of the alley, chat, and then move slowly on.

It was amazing. The same two Normies.

'That's amazing,' he whispered, as they all came out from their hiding places. 'It's always the same two. I've seen them loads of times.'

The man laughed again.

'Six eights are forty-eight,' he said, brushing orange peel off his trouserleg.

'What do you mean?' asked Dolores.

He began to laugh again and then saw their faces and stopped.

'You really don't know, do you?' he said. 'You really were born on The Heights, you're a princess, look at your clothes, look what you're doing, you're some sort of magico and you haven't got a clue.'

Otto had decided that he didn't like the thin man.

Dolores tilted her chin in the air.

'I won't argue with you,' she said with dignity. 'My family is in danger. We have to get to HighNoon. If you people help one another as they say you do, perhaps

you will be so kind as to give me any advice you can.'

'You people,' mimicked the man, 'you people . . .'

'I'm sorry,' she interrupted, 'all this is very new to me.'

'Well, that's obvious.'

'Mum,' said Otto, 'let's keep walking, we can get there.'

They started to walk again and, uninvited, the man came with them.

'I'm Nathaniel Crane,' he said. 'Clockmaker and cat agent. I won't ask who you are. I can smell you. It's my nature. You're a widge who doesn't know anything about widges, aren't you? And this unicorn is probably a widge too, resting, as you might say. And this cat I recognize from way back, I never forget a cat. Shinnabac, isn't it?'

Shinnabac narrowed his eyes. He was not given to a lot of facial expressions.

They rounded a corner and were on a short street leading to the Boulevard.

An empty tram went past.

'There's your answer,' said Nathaniel, 'a tram.'

'Let's just walk,' said Otto.

'I don't think we can take my, a donkey on a tram,' said Dolores.

'There's probably just the driver,' said Nathaniel. 'Leave the driver to me. Find a stop for HighNoon. They come down here, don't they?'

Soon they were assembled at a tram stop. There was a poster stuck there.

IMPOSSIBLE LIST –
NEW EDITION OUT NOW.
REWARD FOR ANY CATS OR BUTTERFLIES
DELIVERED TO THE TOWN HALL.
SPECIAL REWARD FOR MIDSUMMER
BUTTERFLIES.

This street was busier. Several people walked past. They stared at Granny Culpepper. Somebody shouted something about getting back to the mud towns where they belonged.

Otto jiggled the buggy. Standing still was definitely worse than moving on.

'Like your haircut,' said Nathaniel, 'bit of a change from when I saw you last.'

Otto ignored him.

'Let's just walk, Mum,' he said for the third time. 'Those Normies went the other way. No one else will recognize me.'

'Those Normies. THOSE Normies,' whispered Nathaniel scornfully. 'There you go again. Look, six eights are forty-eight. You know Alice, don't you? Alice and Fumi who teach the kids to read? Who teach *all* the kids? They're both

multiples. Get it? Alice is a multiple. So is Fumi. All the Alices are Alice and all the Fumis are Fumi. They multiply themselves together. At night there's just one Alice and one Fumi again. Same with the Normies. There's only two. Mr Six and Mr Eight. Both multiples. They just multiply together like Alice and Fumi. Get everywhere. All over the City at the same time. Same two. Get it? Something happens to Mr Six, all the other Mr Sixes know about it and remember it. Same with Mr Eight. They're magicos working for the enemy. Alice was arrested, by the way.'

While Otto was still trying to think about this a tram rumbled towards them.

Nathaniel put his hand out to stop it. Otto saw that his fingernails were short and extremely pointed.

Two more Normies came patrolling slowly down the street.

'Let's do it,' whispered Dolores to Otto. 'There's no one else on there.'

Nathaniel was already chatting to the driver. He had opened his tattered jacket and was showing him something inside. Otto caught a glimpse of gleaming gold watches pinned on to the lining.

'Is that a horse?' shouted the driver, looking over Nathaniel's bony shoulder.

'Donkey,' said Dolores. And added, in as confident a voice

as she could, 'We usually get two tickets for her because she takes up a bit of room.'

Granny Culpepper was taking up a bit of room now. She squeezed up the steps and along the gangway of the tram, snorting crossly. Her hat fell off completely and was frantically crammed back on her head by Otto.

'Ganny! Ganny!' shouted the twins, who had woken up.

Dolores paid the driver, who couldn't take his eyes off Nathaniel's jacket.

'This is a real bargain,' said Nathaniel, as they set off. 'Tells the time and predicts what sort of day you're going to have. If this light starts flashing you just don't get up at all.'

'We haven't been paid this month,' said the driver. 'It's going to start flashing every day when the bills come in.'

In a mumble of sympathy Nathaniel produced another watch which he said the driver might find especially useful.

Dolores and Otto settled at the back of the tram with the twins on their knees.

'. . . detects gold fragments . . .' Otto heard Nathaniel say soothingly. 'Bits dropped all over the place in the old days. Especially in HighNoon, in those old wooden houses.'

The tram had swung on to the Boulevard. They went right past two Normies.

Then another corner and on up into HighNoon.

'Nearly there,' whispered Otto. He could hear Nathaniel

continuing to woo the driver, '. . . cheapest in this range . . . detects when you need a bath . . . but you have to wear it quite high up your wrist. Well, almost in your armpit, for total accuracy.'

'Pearly Oak, please,' shouted Dolores.

This was their stop. Beside the giant Pearly Oak on Pearly Needle Street. Believed to have been the first tree in the City, it had once been split almost to the roots by lightning but had continued to grow, the two halves linked by branches embracing from either side. It was huge, twisted and magnificent.

With some difficulty Granny Culpepper reversed out of the tram and descended the steps beside this venerable landmark. Shinnabac was still clinging loyally to her back, snarling from time to time to relieve his feelings.

'Thank you so much,' said Dolores to the driver who was, it seemed, buying a number of new watches despite having a perfectly good one in the first place.

Nathaniel walked a little way ahead of them up the steep winding lane to the FireBox Launderette. He looked very much like a ginger cat himself, Otto had decided. Yellow eyes, red gold hair, mysterious bands of freckles almost like stripes. A quick glance up and down the quiet shop fronts and the jumble of overhanging bay windows, sniffing the air.

'I'll just say greetings to Madame le Grey,' he said now,

'then I must be off, princess. I found her a great cat, very successful match, Pinfracca. She's got a soft spot for Nathaniel, has Madame le G.'

Otto pulled a face.

The launderette was closed of course, but lit by a number of candles.

'Wash your cares away,' whispered Dolores, reading the window. 'Today and every day.'

Otto rang the bell hard, desperate to get in and much looking forward to saying goodbye to Nathaniel.

A tall figure in a candlewick dressing gown appeared among the machines. She opened the door and the street lamps glowed on her black face, her grey eyes and the many tiny shells twinkling in her hair.

'Greetings,' said Madame Morgan le Grey. Her voice was as Otto remembered it, serious and stern.

'Good evening, I'm so sorry to disturb you at this hour,' said Dolores. 'Miss Freeze advised us to come here.'

'Miss Fringe,' said Otto.

'Fridge,' said Dolores.

But Madame le Grey, with a nod to Dolores and Otto, had walked up to Granny Culpepper, removed her hat, and bowed solemnly and respectfully. Granny Culpepper bent her graceful neck in response. She really was a very beautiful unicorn.

'You are all welcome,' she said, turning to Dolores. 'And greetings to you, Nathaniel Crane.'

At that moment a slender cat arrived, half the size of Shinnabac in all respects except her ears, which were enormous. She ran to Nathaniel and rubbed against his legs.

'Pinfracca, you rascal,' he said.

Otto heard a hiss somewhere. The hiss of a street-cleaning machine.

'Mum!' he cried. 'They're coming!'

No one argued.

Within the wink of a cat's eye Morgan le Grey had helped Dolores get the buggy through the door. Granny Culpepper followed, stumbling slightly on the step, Shinnabac spitting with alarm.

'But Mr Crane . . .' said Otto, despite himself, as Morgan locked the door and hurried them through the launderette.

'Don't worry about him,' she answered, 'he looks after himself.'

Last to go through the door in the panelled wall, Otto looked back and saw the street cleaner go past with the two Normies on board. Mr Six and Mr Eight.

A ginger cat caught his eye, darting into a doorway on the far side of the road. Must be Madame Morgan's cat, Pin-whatsit. But as they all went into the sitting room with its wonderful inviting velvety sofas, Otto saw Pinfracca sitting on Morgan's shoulder. So it couldn't have been her after all.

'I'm Dolores Hush,' said Dolores. 'My husband is Albert,' she looked firmly at Morgan. 'We were advised to come here by Miss, by a colleague of his, this unicorn is my mother, this is my son Otto, these are . . .'

'Please,' said Morgan le Grey, 'you are safe now. Sit down.'

WAKING AT Morgan's

'Dad!'

Otto was trying to shout. He opened his mouth, flung the whole weight of his body behind the sound. But no sound came.

He sat up, shaking. And opened his eyes.

'Dad?' he whispered.

The room was quiet. His mother and the twins were breathing softly. Zebbie on the sofa, Dolores on the floor with Hepzie snuggled into her neck.

Otto himself was on another sofa. There were cushions and quilts everywhere. The walls were plum-coloured and sunlight seeped around the curtains.

'Would you like breakfast?' asked a voice.

He jumped.

Morgan le Grey had somehow come in silently behind him.

'Come in the kitchen,' she added, 'so we don't disturb the others. Your granny and I are having a chat.'

Otto followed her, picking his way. His head still echoing with the dream about Albert.

The kitchen was full of sunshine and blue and white tiles. Shinnabac sat smugly on an armchair in the corner.

Granny Culpepper, in her human form, was at the table drinking from a large mug. Seeing her there made him realize how much he had preferred her as a unicorn.

'Otto,' she said, 'how nice to see you.'

This was very strange. But then so was everything else.

'Your grandmother re-arranged during the night,' said Morgan, offering him some toast. 'She seems quite refreshed.' And for some reason, and much to Otto's surprise, she gave him a friendly wink.

'I feel wonderful,' exclaimed Granny Culpepper, 'I feel just like a young woman again, all those years being so Normal, such a strain,' she slurped her tea noisily, 'such a strain. You'll love the twins, Madame Morgan, so light, so buoyant, so carefree.'

'My dad's disappeared,' said Otto, not hungry after all.

Behind him Morgan put one hand on each of his shoulders. Her hands felt very strong. It was more of a grip.

'The main thing this morning is that you are all here and safe, which is what your father wanted. I'm sure he will do the best he can, it isn't his fault that he is not best suited—'

'He's got something he has to work on, like a riddle, he's going to solve it.' Otto glared at them both, daring them to argue.

The two women said nothing. Then there was a murmur of voices from the next room as Dolores and the twins woke up.

A Trip on a Carpet

After a little while Otto wandered out into the garden. It was small, with old high walls and lots of flowers. He sat down as far from the house as possible, which wasn't terribly far, and thought about Albert and Alice and Granny Culpepper, everyone who had turned out not to be what he thought they were.

'I must be magico too, in a way,' he said to himself. He couldn't fly like his sisters though. Colours didn't fill the room when he was upset. Papers didn't fly up to his waiting fingers. Was Dolores really a widge? They were different. They cast spells using cats to help them. The cats amplified, whatever that meant.

He went back into the house and through into the

launderette. The machines and the driers were silent. Closed due to Staff Absence. Outside, however, the narrow street was busy. There was a new Town Hall poster on display in the window of the shop opposite.

WANTED
ALBERT HUSH
DANGEROUS LIBRARIAN IMPOSTOR
ALL INFORMATION WILL BE TREATED
IN CONFIDENCE

There was a picture underneath, rather blurred.

A number of people had stopped to look. A couple of sheep joined them and then moved on. Someone else moved on too. A small girl in a baggy black dress with something rolled up under her arm.

She crossed the street and came straight to the launderette.

It was Mab.

He unbolted the door.

A woman pushing a pram stopped beside her just as she was coming in.

'You're from the mud towns, aren't you, love?' she whispered. 'Don't hang around here by yourself, there's a lot of ignorant people about. We don't all believe in this holes in the road business you know, but there's plenty that do.'

A Trip on a Carpet

'May we meet again on a better day,' replied Mab. 'Is that bread baking?' she asked as soon as she was inside.

He hadn't noticed until now but there was a smell of bread, probably Granny Culpepper who couldn't stop being busy.

'No matter,' Mab snapped, 'no matter, we've got to get going. Make some excuses to your dear mummy.'

'Where to? Why? Not on the mat?'

'It won't take long. It's very important. We'll take off from the garden. I'll go round and wait for you.'

'How did you know there is a garden? How did you know there's a door in the wall?'

'Just hurry. I've been flying over this City all my life, remember. Have you had breakfast?'

Why did she keep on talking about food? 'Sure, yes.'

'Fine, fine, see you round the back in a minute.'

He wrote a note to say that he would be back soon and not to worry, and put it on the mantelpiece in the sitting room behind a large glass ball.

Mab was waiting for him impatiently under the rowan tree.

Why did the carpet have to be so small?

It lifted, turned, brushed the tops of some golden flowers and then climbed steeply. Other gardens and the lanes of HighNoon spread out like patchwork. The City glinted in the summer haze. Crate birds were gliding in majestic circles. Riding the warm air rising, barely moving their wings.

There was the Boulevard, the Karmidee Tower, the Town Hall, then further down, Dealer's Square and the bright tents of the street markets.

Over the park, the steamy tropical corner with parrots in the treetops, the snowy skating rink, the extremely bouncy trampolines, the slide that went right out of the park, along several streets and back in again.

He even picked out Parry Street.

And everywhere trees. And green roof gardens.

Wherever were they going?

Of course, the Whispering Park. The strange place she'd brought him. It seemed years ago.

They dipped sharply, he closed his eyes and they landed with a thud on the mossy grass.

'I told you he'd come,' said Mab.

'Why's he lying down?' someone else asked.

'Motion sickness,' said another voice.

Laughter.

Otto crawled off the carpet and sat down. His legs felt wobbly.

Three figures were looming around him. Two other children, bigger and older than himself and Mab.

'Thanks for coming, Otts,' she said coolly. 'Interesting haircut.'

There was a boy with shells woven into his hair like

A Trip on a Carpet

Madame Morgan, and a girl with the same purple shadows under her eyes as Mab.

'This is Amos and this is Lydia,' said Mab. 'They want to know if you're one of us or one of them.'

'Why?' asked Otto, as calm as he could make it.

'Because if you're one of us,' said the boy, 'you might be able to help. You're a citizen. We're not.'

'We want to stop what's happening,' said Mab.

'Let's not say any more,' said the girl. 'Do the test.'

For a moment Otto thought of jumping for the carpet. But of course it was hers. It wouldn't take him anywhere now.

'The test,' said the girl again.

'Otto,' said Mab, 'do you remember coming here before?'

He stared at her and raised his eyebrows. She sounded like an adult talking to a baby.

'We walked all around,' she continued, flushing slightly. 'Do you remember the fish, you walked under them and they moved and you said it must be the wind.'

He went on staring.

'Look, that's all it is, just walk under them again so the others can see what happens OK?'

'He's not very helpful so far,' said the girl.

'Otto, please,' whispered Mab, 'they don't believe me.'

He followed her through the park and they came to the shoal of fish. It looked very beautiful in the sunshine.

'Just walk under it,' said Mab.

'I didn't trick you that night,' he whispered back, 'it wasn't a trap. I tried to save you.'

'You did save me,' she said quietly. 'You've saved me twice.'

'What's going on?' asked the boy.

'Just walk under it,' said Mab again.

Otto walked under the floating fish. When he was right underneath he realized that they were beginning to tremble. Then there was a flash of reflected sunlight as they turned, bright as knives, and faced the opposite way and went on turning, right round, back where they started.

Then they were still again and he was out the other side.

He looked at the other children and they were all looking at him.

'360,' said the boy with the shells softly.

'Now do you believe me?' demanded Mab.

'OK, OK, you were right.'

'This is it, Otto,' said Mab, 'there isn't much time. Our people are in danger, we are becoming like slaves—'

'We're supposed to have a King,' snapped the older girl.

'Yeah, right,' said Amos, keeping his eyes on Otto.

'We'd just about written him off,' continued Mab, 'but then we had the idea of trying to find him, us three, I mean.'

'No one else can see the point,' said Amos. 'But we want to offer him our help. We're the only ones with mats. We fly a lot, especially at night, we could be like spies, take messages. We thought you might know where he is.'

They all looked at Otto.

'What makes you think that?'

'Don't you?' said Mab, very cold again.

'No, I don't.'

'Well that's strange,' said Amos, 'seeing as how he's your dad and all.'

They knew, then. Of course, he'd told her Albert's name before he knew what it might mean.

'They tried to arrest him at the library,' Otto blurted. 'I don't know what happened. I think he got away. They searched our flat. My family had to escape. We're at someone else's place now. But he's working on something, there's something he's trying to do.'

'My dad's disappeared too,' said Amos and a blue haze flickered around him and was gone.

'When he was saying goodbye all these colours came into the room,' said Otto, 'blues and greens, all up the walls.'

'Some of us are like that. You learn to control it as you get older. Hide your feelings. He probably just didn't want to hide them any more.'

'But it's incredible. Why do you hide it?'

Mab rolled her eyes and the others laughed.

'Maybe we didn't in the beginning before the Normals

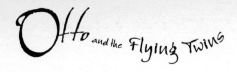

came,' she said, 'but everyone says it's primitive now. There's lots of things like that. Energy. Lydia here is an artist.'

'A painter?'

'No, not a painter, Mr Normal, just watch. Go on, Lydia.'

The girl looked at Otto. 'It's not funny to us,' she said.

'I'm not laughing,' said Otto.

Lydia stood up and raised her arms.

'Go on,' said Mab.

'I'm thinking . . . I know . . . a present for our small friend here . . .'

Something seemed to be happening on the parched grass next to Otto. A brown shape, a glint of scales, Otto smelt smoke. He stood up quickly.

'It's OK,' hissed Mab.

The shape grew. It writhed in the air. Clawed feet reached down. More smoke and Otto coughed. It was FireBox. Green, gold and purple. Standing right there next to him. Much closer than he'd seen him that night at the launderette. His eyes were almost luminous with long thick lashes. His tongue dark green, glowing with cinders.

'Brilliant,' whispered Mab.

FireBox suddenly spread his wings and flapped them, he tilted back his great head and breathed a flame into the air. The heat touched Otto's face.

Lydia lowered her arms and sat down heavily.

The dragon began to fade, back into a brown cloud. Then only smoke and then just the taste of smoke on Otto's lips.

Lydia didn't seem to want to look at Otto. He realised that she was shy.

'That's FireBox,' said Otto respectfully into the silence.

'I don't want to have to do that for crowds of citizens every night,' said Lydia. 'I don't want to be in a freak show.'

More silence.

'I've seen that dragon before,' said Otto. 'My dad gave it some medicine or something, made it better anyway, when it was sick.'

'That's why I painted him,' said Lydia. 'Because your father is good with animals. Especially our sort, wild ones and Impossible ones.'

At the word 'Impossible' they all laughed except Otto.

'How do you know that about him?'

'There's always been rumours,' said Mab, 'and there was a Karmidee whose job it was to keep an eye on him, sort of protect him, although he didn't know it. Your father fell out with *his* father when he became a sleeper, you see, his father wanted him to stay in the mud towns, but his mother found this distant cousin who was also interested in books or whatever and she became a sleeper too, someone at the library—'

'Miss Fringe!' exclaimed Otto. 'Miss Fringe is a Karmidee and she was there at the library to protect him and he didn't know!'

He caught the three of them glancing quickly at each other.

'We're going to tell you everything now,' said Mab. 'We know he escaped. Miss Fringe went with him. He gave her some message for his family. Then he told her to go. He said it was better that way. She's the one who told us where you were.'

'We got the message,' said Otto. 'She brought the message, but it was very hard for her to talk to us, why didn't you tell me he'd escaped? What else do you know that you're not saying?'

'Nothing, that's all,' said Mab.

'Well, where is Miss Fridge?'

'Fringe. Hiding. Her place in the City was searched. She went back to TigerHouse. That's how we got to hear about it. But she won't say any more and now she's disappeared again.'

'So if she's supposed to help him why did she leave him alone?'

'Oh, Otto,' said Mab.

'He is the King of the Karmidee,' said Lydia simply, 'and he asked her to go.'

Otto put his head in his hands.

For a moment no one spoke. Amos went to put his

arm around his shoulders and Otto shook him off without looking up.

'And why,' he asked, 'did you bring me to your stupid park and make me walk under your stupid, stupid fish?'

He took his hands away and his eyes were streaming.

'Because Mab saw what happened before. And we needed to be sure that you are who you are.'

'To be sure I'm Otto Hush of 15 Hershell Buildings, Parry Street?'

'To be sure that you are a Karmidee. And not just a Karmidee, one with great energy, the son of a King.'

'Watch me,' said Mab, and she stood up and went over to the fish. Slowly she walked underneath. They turned, just as they had done for Otto, but only half as far.

'I'm 180,' she said, 'all three of us are. The energy round you is very strong.'

'No it isn't. I can't do anything.'

'Some abilities don't manifest easily, especially rare ones from the old days, like heartsight,' said Lydia, looking thoughtfully at Otto.

'So what's that then?'

'Seeing into people's hearts, seeing the things they've shut away inside. My great-great-grandfather was supposed to have had heartsight, so they say, but I haven't heard of anybody since.'

'You're 360, Mr Small,' said Amos, 'and that's big. Maybe you just don't know yourself very well yet.'

'And now we have to go,' said Mab, 'and you have to come too. That way, when the King summons you, you will have plenty to tell him.'

Amos had a bag over his shoulder. Slowly and carefully, he took something out. Something faded and dusty and worn.

He put it on the ground and unrolled it.

'For you,' he said.

Otto's mouth fell open. 'For me, for my own?'

It was a mat like Mab's, covered in the same pattern of butterflies.

'A family heirloom,' said Amos. 'Yours to keep now.'

'But—'

'Hurry up and get on it,' said Mab.

Amos and Lydia were getting ready to fly. A moment later they were soaring up over the park.

'Hurry up,' yelled Mab, sailing after them.

'Thank you!' called Otto.

Without giving himself time to think he sat on his carpet and pulled at the fringe. With a sickening lunge into the air, too fast and too steep, he was following the others.

They were heading across the City. The mud towns, of course. Otto was rigid. He couldn't look down. Just let it be over soon.

Red Moon

They landed on wasteland.

'Take these,' said Amos, pulling some things out of his bag. It was a green and black patchwork coat and a wide brimmed hat with a band of shells around it.

'To cover you up,' he said.

Otto put them on.

'Remember to keep your mouth shut,' said Mab.

'Where are we going?'

'I'm going to show you around.'

The hat and coat smelt of wood smoke and musty spices. He remembered pulling the mobile away from Mab's face when she had crashed in through his window. He had first smelt this smell then. Magico. Magical.

'Are we going to your house?' he asked her now.

'No,' she said quickly, 'I live in TigerHouse. This is Red Moon.'

They took a path along the river. A boat passed them, going upstream towards the mountains. There seemed to be a family on board, with bags and parcels and chickens packed in too.

Mab turned and said quietly to Otto, 'They're leaving, going up to the caves in the mountains in the north. Quite a few families are hiding up there.'

They had reached the first of the stilt houses, which were covered in carvings of animals and birds, a bit like the ones on the Karmidee Tower.

'Look!' said Lydia, pointing to a jetty below them. It seemed to Otto to be covered in broken glass.

'They were here last night,' said Amos.

A woman came out of the nearest house, onto the deck that ran all around it. She was carrying a child of about three years old.

'Honourable greetings, sister, what happened here?' called Amos.

'They took my husband,' she said. 'We refused the money.'

She seemed about to cry but something else happened instead. The child, a girl, threw back her head and there was a crackling and sparking in the air.

It was ice. Ice crystallized and spreading all around her.

'Don't give up hope!' cried Mab. 'The King has not forgotten us.'

'The King!' spat the woman. 'Where is he? What is he doing? Reading a book about it?'

Otto started to speak and Mab stopped him with a look. Not so clever to sound like a citizen here. They went on.

Most of the houses were empty. In places there were signs that people had left in a hurry, or been forced to leave. Doors stood open, possessions, shoes, unfinished carvings and tools were scattered around. Small dragons, presumably babies, scavenged in the rubbish.

Out in the middle of the river the houses clustered round a large platform and the children went up there, along the creaking walkways.

People were sitting hunched, some arguing, others very quiet, dazed-out and dozing.

'I say take the money and go and work for them,' said a man with dragon tattoos on his face.

'Perform! Do tricks for the rest of your life?' This was a woman speaking. A unicorn sat beside her with its head on her lap.

'If we don't they'll just arrest us anyway. And it's a living. It's not safe to try and sell stuff in the City any more, she's turned them all against us with her crazy talk about holes and mines—'

'Have you any idea what will happen to you if you have to keep using your energy night after night, week after week? You'll be wrecked in a year. It'll kill you—'

'So what's your suggestion, die in prison? Or are you mad enough to try and fight them, like those poor bastards last night?'

'The Normals are cursed. They always want something and that's where their energy goes, searching, wanting, hungering and hating. We're different—'

'Six and Eight don't seem so different,' snarled someone else. 'Treacherous, two-faced, double-crossing—'

The speaker saw Amos and Lydia and raised his hand. 'Honourable greetings to our young mat-flyers. Any news? Still wasting time looking for our leader?' He made a snoring noise and there was sarcastic laughter all round.

Mab pulled Otto away back to the path, picking their way past people who seemed to be wandering restlessly from house to house.

'Remember everything you've seen,' said Mab, 'to tell the King.'

'Is Miss Fringe here?'

'TigerHouse, but I think she was going to leave for the caves last night.'

Otto thought of his mysterious grandfather with the bitter granite face.

Maybe he was here now, in one of these houses . . .

'Can we—'

'Ssh! Keep your voice down, Mr Normal, some citizens came down here last night trying to help, bringing food and stuff and they got thrown in the river. Can you swim?'

Two children were playing on the bank. A handful of twigs was spinning in the air in front of them.

'Higher! Higher!' said the boy.

The twigs did go higher, wobbled and then crashed on to the ground.

'Who's your friend, Mab?' said the girl.

'Cousin,' said Mab, hurrying Otto along.

Soon she stopped and unrolled her mat. Otto, grim-faced, did the same.

THE Arena

'Try to be less stiff, relax, think of the mat as part of you,' called Mab.

Ho. Ho. Ho.

They crossed the City again. Heading for the mountain in the west known as CrabFace. The prison was there, in more caves used first by the Karmidee. Lower down where the mountain reached the valley floor Otto made out a new building, on land that used to be a park.

'The arena,' shouted Mab, her hair flying. 'Come lower.'

She steered downwards, making it look easy as ever, and Otto followed, making it look difficult.

The arena was almost finished. In the middle there was a huge stage where the magicos would presumably be performing, and tiered seats rose up all around, as tall as the Town Hall.

Posters were already in place along the sides.

MAGICO SHOWS TWICE DAILY
RAINBOWS OF COLOUR!
PICTURES IN THE AIR!
ICE! FIRE! DRAGONS! A FLYING CHILD!
AND MUCH MUCH MORE!

'And that's where they're going to live,' called Mab, floating next to him. 'And stop gritting your teeth.'

The magicos were going to live in rows of cheap looking huts, some on wheels, some built specially, some still being built now. Workmen hurried back and forth.

'Don't go too low, look down there.'

Families were sitting around campfires. Magicos. Imprisoned by a high wire fence patrolled by Normies with dogs.

Red Moon had been a cruel sight but this was far worse.

'They give them free bloodberry juice and three meals a day,' said Mab, 'and they are still building more huts over there.'

Just then a Normie looked up and saw them.

'Up!' yelled Mab.

The Normies started shouting. One of them fired a net. The dogs barked. Now magicos were shouting too, encouragement to the little figures in the sky. As the Normie with the net went to fire again a magico man jumped on him and knocked him to the ground. Screams and fighting. More Normies running.

'We're going to get you out!' cried Otto. Ice and sparks and rainbows were exploding all over the site, just as the cruel posters promised they would do in the arena.

'Not that high!' screamed Mab somewhere.

He looked frantically around for her but there was nothing. Wet whiteness. He was in a cloud.

Teeth chattering he dipped down again. More cloud. He looped round the way he had come. If it was that way. More whiteness and it seemed hard to think and then suddenly he was out of it.

'Get back here, you stupid Normal Respectable—'

For once she looked frightened herself.

They flew without speaking over parts of the City he didn't recognize, and the sun began to dry the cloud from his face.

THE Mountain

'And now we've got one more thing to show you, and it's the worst thing of all,' said Mab. 'I'm not sure you're tough enough to handle it.'

They were climbing higher, towards the highest of the ring of mountains, the great and sinister BrokenHeart. It was forest below them now. Otto saw a band of wolves running across a clearing and then he made out a stony track, almost overgrown in places.

'Mab,' he called. He was scared of something he couldn't name.

The air closer to BrokenHeart was cold. The mountainside rose out of the trees, the trees clung on a little way further and then there was heather and then rocks. A grey bird with a

beak like a hook soared past Otto's mat and gave a piercing
screaming cry that nearly flung him into the gaping landscape
below.

Now he saw that the mountain looked as if it had been cut
open. A narrow crevasse ran from the peak, under clouds,
down into the trees.

Mab was spiralling down and he followed her, tilting his mat
more than he intended, yelling with fright, and heard his
voice returned like another child calling back.

A wind was howling through the wound in the mountain.
He fought to steer the mat.

Down and down they went until at last she hovered just
above the trees.

'We can't stay long,' she said, as soon as he was beside her.
'They might see us.'

'They? Who?'

She beckoned him to follow her towards the dark opening
between the two terrible walls of rock.

'There, look, on the OTHER SIDE.'

The wind was blasting into his face. He could see her in
front of him, her white hair streaming, like a tiny insect,
bobbing and advancing further and further into the icy dark.

He followed her.

And at last, below in the gloom he saw that the pass was

blocked by a great stone arch, enclosing what looked like two massive wooden doors.

Beyond, on the other side, he thought he could make out some goats on the floor of the chasm. He had seen some higher up in the mountains along the tree line.

But they weren't goats. They were people.

He tried to get closer.

Men, how many, ten, fifteen, with pickaxes and barrows and shovels . . .

Suddenly the wind caught his mat underneath somehow and lifted it up and backwards. It turned over, him clinging on, and came back the right way up, still careering out of control through the air and out of the mountain back into the valley. He was screaming for Mab as it dropped like a stone and then swung sideways over the trees again.

She was next to him.

'Are you OK?' she shouted through the wind.

He nodded, swallowing mouthfuls of air.

'Tell the King we saw them when we were flying one night. They must have got out by the secret tunnels and come round. The Gates are still shut. Tell him it looks as if they're clearing the road on the *other side*. The road through the pass. The road to Araminta's Gates.'

Otto heard her. Then he steered his mat down between the pine trees.

She was shouting to him to come back. He ignored this.

He landed and staggered off into the shadows to be sick.

When he had finished and he seemed to have vomited most of what he'd eaten in the last year he rolled up his mat and set off shakily through the trees. Then he sat down for a while.

He didn't want to talk to anyone.

The forest floor was lit by bands of sunlight. Lemon, gold and green. Birds sang in the trees. It was a different world from the one above, the one in which he had just almost been killed, and he decided to stay down there forever.

Mab was calling him, flying backwards and forwards.

After a while his legs felt more as they were supposed to feel. He stood up. He knew he'd have to get back on the mat but, to give himself some more time, he went to look for the stony road to the Gates.

He found the road and followed it. Abruptly it led into shadow and then into the chasm itself. And then, when the towering walls on either side seemed to be falling on him and he was ready to turn and run, he saw Araminta's Gates and they were something to see indeed.

They were, Otto thought, as tall as Hershell Buildings. Two great Gates, made from solid wood bolted together by massive iron studs. More iron, wrought into a lavish pattern of curls and loops, twisted over the surface and depicted a tree, one side of the trunk on each of the Gates.

There was an enormous handle on one Gate that had been worn bright at the bottom, presumably where people had held it to pull it downwards. Apart from this, however, there was no sign that anything there had been disturbed for a very long time. Sandy dirt, blown by the wind maybe, had drifted along the ground against the base of the Gates.

There were no plants, no grass. Not enough light.

Otto was about to go closer when he heard voices and footsteps somewhere behind him.

He looked for a hiding place and then made a run for the trees, diving out of sight just as two men and a horse came down the road towards him.

The horror of nearly falling off the mat hadn't left Otto. It seemed to him that there was danger everywhere.

The two men however were not dangerous. Neither was their long-suffering horse.

It was Councillors Trim and Tapper, released from prison by Mayor Crumb to make good by successfully travelling to the Outside and gathering information about the Normal world.

Otto recognized them. He decided to try and follow, fully expecting, as any citizen would, to see them open the giant Gates, go through and close them behind them. After all,

everyone knew that they could go Outside if they wanted.

He crept noisily through the trees and the wind in the chasm above carried their voices to him. Then as they entered the mountain he trailed them, keeping close to the rock, relying on his mat to save him if necessary.

'Have you got the maps?' asked Councillor Trim, not, it seemed, for the first time.

'Yes, yes, yes,' snapped Councillor Tapper. 'Have YOU got the emergency rations?'

'Yes, yes, yes.'

'Well then.'

'Well, then.'

'It's the worst possible time for me to have to go on some stupid trip abroad,' said Councillor Trim. 'Everyone will be coming into the shop wanting their winter shoes and boots before we get back. I've left my brother-in-law in charge but really, he's a good shoe-maker but he loses his temper if the customers can't make up their minds quickly—'

'I KNOW about your brother-in-law,' growled Councillor Tapper. 'I have just spent two nights in a dark, wet, dirty prison cell hearing about him. I don't want to go either. We shall miss all sorts of important Council Meetings. Now, let's just go over everything one last time.'

They had arrived at the doors and they looked very small beside them. Even the horse looked small.

'It's cold here, isn't it?' said Councillor Trim.

'We have maps, money, emergency rations, notebooks and lists of things to look out for and check up on.'

'Yes.'

'We will use Nostrillisimus for the first part of the journey, which is across some sort of wasteland or whatever. When we find a road of a suitable size we will undoubtedly be able to catch a tram to the big cities on the Outside.'

'Some people say that there are carriages that go to the moon,' said Councilor Trim wistfully.

'I've never believed that,' said Councillor Tapper firmly, 'and I have a fear of flying, it brings on my indigestion just thinking about it.'

'Now, what did Mayor Crumb say when in his most generous Mayorfulness he came to the prison and allowed us to come out of that horrible dank dark cell?'

'He said we must succeed in our mission and that if we did not return, in six weeks, with our notebooks full of notes about what is Normal and what is Respectable and what is Impossible—'

'Yes, yes.'

'We'll be back in prison and he'll throw away the key. He asked us to make this trip before and we let him down.'

They both fell silent. Nostrillisimus rattled his bridle.

'But neither of us remember him asking us, do we?'

'No.'

Another pause.

'Well we won't let him down this time then,' said Councillor Tapper. 'Let's sing a verse of the new City Anthem before we go.'

They began to sing lustily, a small sound in that roofless, mocking place.

> 'There is nothing so Normal as Normal,
> To be Normal is everything,
> We are proud to be Normal as Normal
> And so we proudly sing
> Be Normal, be Normal, be Normal,
> Let Normal be your aim . . .'

A grey bird, like the one that had screamed at Otto, swooped over the Gates and screamed at the two Councillors.

Nostrillisimus reared in fright and the remainder of the anthem was abandoned abruptly.

'Councillor Trim,' gasped Councillor Tapper, hanging on to Nostrillisimus with difficulty, 'if you would be so kind as to open the, er, Gates.'

But the handle was very high and, eventually, when Nostrillisimus was calmed, Councillor Trim had to climb on to his back and stand up in order to reach it.

Otto held his breath. He was about to see the huge Gates open.

Except he wasn't.

Councillor Trim swung his weight on the handle and it came down towards him. Then, inexplicably, he let go.

'Go on!' shouted Councillor Tapper.

Councillor Trim did not go on, however, instead he climbed silently down off the horse with an extremely strange expression on his face.

'Oh, I'll do it!' exclaimed Councillor Tapper.

Very soon he too was swinging on the handle and then, just like Councillor Trim, he let go and, in a daze, came back down to the ground.

The two Councillors stood there. Then they looked around. The Gates, the mountain, everything around them seemed to amaze them.

'What are we doing here?' whispered Councillor Tapper. 'Where are we?'

'I don't like it,' whispered Councillor Trim. 'Did we come for a walk or something? Is this your horse? Are these our bags? Why have we got all these bags?'

As Otto watched in amazement, they turned away from the Gates and began to walk slowly towards him. He stayed where he was and Councillor Trim saw him.

'Are you on your own?' he asked. 'This isn't a very nice

place for children. I should go home if I were you.'

Nostrillisimus gave Otto a baleful glance and stomped past.

As they continued back out of the mountain, with Otto behind them, their conversation became more cheerful.

'I'm going to the shop, why not come and have a cup of tea,' said Councillor Trim. 'I want to get back because I've had to leave my brother-in-law in charge.'

'This horse must be lost, he's following me,' said Councillor Tapper. 'Do we often go for walks together like this? Why did we go to that terrible place?'

Otto saw Mab. She had landed in the forest and was beckoning to him. He made his way towards her.

'Did you touch the handle on the Gates?' she demanded at once.

'Of course not.' How could he anyway? It was far too high.

'Thank goodness. I suddenly thought you might not know about it.'

'Know about what?'

'The handle, Araminta's Gates, the whole thing, your father told you, did he?'

Tempted to pretend, Otto decided at the last minute not to after all.

'Not really, no. I've never seen this place before. Those two men were going to open the Gates but they seemed to change their minds or something.'

The Mountain

'Yet another thing you don't know, Mr Citizen. A Karmidee Queen, born with the mark, you know about that at least, she built these Gates. When citizens decide to leave and get hold of that handle they forget why they came down to the Gates at all. On the other side there's some sort of illusion apparently. The Gates look like part of the mountain.'

'So how did that help?'

'Think about it. People stopped leaving and people stopped arriving. Gradually the Outside forgot about us. No more being taken away to be in freak shows.'

'So what happens if a magico, a Karmidee, gets hold of that handle?'

'Same thing, but we don't because we know. And anyway, we don't want to leave very often. This is the only safe place in the world for us. There are some tunnels, if it's really necessary.'

'And what about the Tourist Information Office?'

'The people who work there just keep telling the Town Hall that the City has visitors. It's all run by Karmidee. Same with the Boulevard Hotel. Araminta's idea.'

He stared at her.

Then past her. Into his own spinning thoughts.

'Otto?'

'I've, I've got to get back, my dad might——'

'I know. Are you OK to fly?' She'd seen him nearly come off the mat.

He nodded, not feeling OK at all. 'Let's go now, Mab.'

The return flight was easier than the one to the mountain. She came part of the way with him and pointed out HighNoon and then wheeled away towards the mud towns as he set off for the launderette.

Communicating

He landed in the garden and as he walked in through the kitchen door Dolores seized him and pushed him to a chair.

'Oh, Ottie, where on earth did you go? You mustn't go walking the streets, you could be arrested just like that and whatever are you wearing?'

'I didn't walk,' said Otto.

'Ottie fly! Ottie fly!' sang Hepzie approvingly.

'Did you, Otto?' asked Granny Culpepper, who was doing the washing-up wearing a daisy chain and numerous other flowers stuck in her hair. 'How exciting and what a lovely hat, it'll be perfect when you've grown into it.'

'Has Dad—' began Otto.

Dolores shook her head.

Otto was about to say more when Morgan le Grey came in from the sitting room carrying the large glass ball which he had seen on the mantelpiece.

'I'm having trouble getting through in there,' she said inexplicably, 'so I'm going to try in here.'

She put the ball down on the kitchen table and pushed the clutter of breakfast things and lunch things and baby toys out of the way.

'Silence, please,' she said.

'Simunce!' cried Zeborah, who was sitting on the floor for once, and under the table.

Otto reached down and picked her up and sneaked a kiss on the top of her head through a flame-coloured riot of hair.

Hepzie hovered over Morgan.

'Calling Madame Honeybun Nicely, calling Madame Honeybun Nicely,' said Morgan, peering into the ball.

'It's a crystal communicator,' said Granny Culpepper cheerfully to Otto.

'Simunce!' sang Zebbie.

Morgan tapped on the crystal communicator rather sharply with a wooden spoon and it lit up all pink.

There was something inside.

'Draw the curtains would you, Dolores,' said Madame Morgan. 'It's very faint.'

Communicating

Now Otto could see something. A crown? A castle? No, a cake. Underneath, in big letters, it said,

The Amazing Cake Shop,
proprietor Madame Honeybun Nicely.
Personalised cakes to order.
Improve your Mood with High Class Food.

'Good, that's her,' said Morgan, 'shameless advertising as usual.'

Then the cake disappeared and there was the face of the curvy woman who had saved him from the Normies.

'Madame Morgan le Grey calling,' said Morgan.

'I can see you, darling,' said the curvy woman in her soft lazy voice, 'no need to explain.'

'I hope we are not disturbing you,' said Madame Morgan, crisply, 'it concerns FireBox. He went off suddenly yesterday and he hasn't come home. It's never happened before.'

Honeybun frowned. In the background Otto made out what looked like a kitchen. A faint and delicious smell of baking cakes seemed to be leaking out of the crystal whatever-it-was and into the room.

'Well, he was here the night before last. You know he sometimes drops into my garden for liquorice buns. He ate about thirty. And there was someone with him. A gentleman

who thought I didn't see him. He hid in the bushes, and jumped back on to FireBox's back just at the last minute and I did notice that he had some sort of bandage on one leg. But you know, Madame Morgan, we don't ask questions these days, do we . . .'

'Would you let us know if you see him again?'

'Yes, darling, of course. Six and Eight keep coming in the shop. It's very worrying. I had to rescue Nathaniel Crane and some little boy from them the other day. They are just everywhere. I may close altogether for a while.'

The conversation went on for a little bit longer but Otto had stopped listening. He was thinking about the man who had hidden in the bushes while FireBox ate the thirty buns. The man with the bandaged leg. He was sure it was Albert.

'Mr Crane is coming here soon,' said Dolores to Otto when the crystal communications were over. 'He is introducing me to a cat.'

'Coming here!' exclaimed Otto.

'I realize you didn't exactly take to him but he did help us.'

'We would have been fine without him. And he was rude to you. And Dad wouldn't like him at all.'

'Your mother must have a cat to amplify for her if she is to become a satisfactory widge,' said Morgan le Grey, 'and the better a widge she is the better for all of us. Cats are the only creatures who can truly empty their brains at will and allow the spells to amplify inside their heads. Mr Crane can judge a cat's potential better than anyone. He has been recruiting cats for over one hundred years.'

Otto could think of no answer to this. In fact he could suddenly hardly think at all. He had seen terrible things, he had nearly been killed by BrokenHeart and he hadn't finished a meal properly for three days. He stood up, swayed and fell dizzily onto the floor.

Albert AND Nathaniel

Albert had thought of trying to escort his family to the safety of the launderette by flying over the route on the dragon, but the danger of actually giving them away rather than protecting them forced him to leave them to make the journey alone.

That night, after he had sent Miss Fringe home, had been the longest of his life. Then, just before dawn, he had learnt that they were safe. It was Nathaniel Crane who told him. FireBox and Albert had settled down to spend the day out of sight among the domes and towers and gables of the mighty Town Hall roof.

Nathaniel came lightly over the tiles in the form of a cat and, seeing Albert and FireBox, had taken on his human form to have a chat, magico to magico.

Albert and Nathaniel

He recounted how he had protected a beautiful woman, a unicorn, a stubborn boy with a mad haircut and some babies. To hear him tell it he'd practically fought the Normies off with his bare hands.

Albert asked no questions, said little. He recognized his family but did not admit it.

'A crazy princess,' said Nathaniel, 'and proud. Didn't seem to know anything about magicos. Crazy.'

'Crazy indeed,' agreed Albert. He knew about widges and unicorns. Despite everything the realization that Granny Culpepper must have been a widge all this time made him laugh out loud.

'It's not funny,' said Nathaniel. 'If it hadn't been for me they'd all have been arrested.'

And Albert stopped laughing again.

'And the most unbelievable thing is that I went back,' continued Nathaniel, relishing the tale, 'I went back when the Normies had gone because I reckoned if this Heights woman has decided to become the widge she really is, with her mother being one and all, well, she's going to need Nathaniel isn't she, to introduce her to a suitable cat. So I go round to the front of the launderette but it's all dark. So I didn't want to disturb them if they were asleep so I crept round the back and had a look in between the curtains. You won't believe what I saw . . .'

Otto and the Flying Twins

Albert had gone very, very pale. Or perhaps it was the grey dawn on his face.

'The little girls were flying all around the kitchen. Bobbing round the ceiling! Beautiful, like little birds. No wonder they're all creeping through the streets like there's a price on their heads! That Elfina whatsit has been sniffing round the muds for days, her and Six and Eight, asking about flying kids and so on. I wouldn't like to be in their shoes. I went home after that. Thought I'd call again another day.'

'Are you sure they were flying?' asked Albert after a moment. 'Perhaps Madame le Grey had just put some sort of spell on them, for a game, just for a little while, before they had their baths.'

'Maybe,' said Nathaniel, who didn't seem to like this less exciting angle on his story. 'But I saw what I saw.'

'I don't think there's been anything like that for a long time,' Albert went on. 'I wonder if it's even possible any more.'

'I saw what I saw,' said Nathaniel, grumpily. 'And what about this King then, supposed to be there when we need him, what do you think about him then? Albert the Librarian they call him.'

Nathaniel laughed. Albert managed a smile.

Nathaniel stayed there a few minutes longer. All around

them the day was coming. The last star faded into the mystery of the sky.

'You staying here, are you?' he asked, stretching unhurriedly, ready for the journey home, like a cat stretches in the morning.

'Probably,' said Albert, 'I'm meeting someone tomorrow night.'

'Honourable greetings, then,' said Nathaniel. And he seemed to fold into himself and to blur, as if Albert saw him through a window streaked with falling rain. Then he was a cat and was gone.

Nathaniel AND Elfina

Although Nathaniel moved swiftly over the rooftops back to SteepSide, in truth he was tired and longing to sleep in his rocking-chair.

He arrived at his shop just as the first trams were starting to creak past up the little street.

Nathaniel Crane, Clockmaker

it said over the door. His bench and tools were just inside the dusty bay window. Customers found it reassuring to be able to see Mr Crane at work. It developed trust. Good for business.

Now, however, he assumed that no one was looking into

the darkened workshop as he changed back into a man and opened the door into the back room.

Here all was cosy and comfortable. A grandfather clock with a tree gilded on its face ticked in the corner. There was a warm tiled stove with a chimney and each of the tiles was decorated with patterns of leaves.

Nathaniel lit the lamps and took something out of the pocket of his velvety coat and placed it very carefully on top of the clock. Then he took off the coat altogether. His waistcoat was a maze of stripes and patches.

He lit the stove to make a cup of raspberry tea.

Soon he would turn back into a cat and curl up for a delicious sleep on his rocking-chair. He had no human bed. Cats sleep better than people.

The kettle began to steam and the clock gave a soft whirr and then burst into life.

'Dong,' it began. 'Dong.' It was six o'clock.

'Hello, Mr Crane,' said a low voice behind him. Almost a whisper. And then the last chime from the clock.

Nathaniel, at the stove, was so amazed that for a moment he stood quite still. In that tiny portion of time he heard the softest creak of the floorboards. He turned very fast, an empty saucepan raised in his hand.

Elfina Crink was standing behind the rocking-chair. She too was holding something in her hand. Something small and

black and shiny that she had taken from on top of the clock.

Nathaniel slowly lowered the saucepan and she smiled.

Still smiling she tossed the strange treasure into the air and it spun upwards.

Nathaniel jumped to catch it. It came to the top of its flight, way up out of reach, and as it slowed it was plain to see that it was a little cat carved from black stone.

Being closely related to a cat even when he was a man, Nathaniel could jump high.

Elfina, however, jumped higher. She was taller, her arms were longer. She caught the cat and clenched her fingers around it without missing a breath.

'Bad luck, Nathaniel,' she said.

His tawny eyes flicked from her hand to her face and back again.

'You'll get it back,' she said. 'I just want you to do something.'

'How did you get in here?'

'My father was a thief, he taught me to pick locks, and it was a little noisy, just for a moment. Dong, dong,' she mimicked, laughing nastily. 'Clocks and trees everywhere I look. Didn't help you this time though. I wasn't always a member of the Council, Nathaniel, I knew you when I was a child, here in SteepSide. I lived here with my father for a while. Right opposite. Saw you coming and going from my window up there. Coming and going and changing, as you might say. Do you remember my father? He didn't like cats much.'

Nathaniel scrabbled through his two hundred years of memories. Saw a glimpse of a hungry-faced girl and a dazed-out man who tried to kick him when he saw him as a cat and complained to him about money and women when he saw him as a man. So that was Elfina. And her father.

'That's my secret,' said Elfina, 'or part of it. You wouldn't know it, would you? I tell them I was born on The Heights and they all believe me. And this is your secret here,' she unclenched the cage of her fingers a little way and the cat gleamed inside it. 'You can't change back without this, can you? I heard all about people like you when I was a kid. This isn't just a carved piece of stone, is it, it's the secret, the secret of your cat energy. The place where you keep it when you are being a man. Your familiar, they call it. It even feels warm, Nathaniel. Just a tiny bit alive. What will you do if I don't give it back? You'll always be just a man. And you'll grow old.'

He licked his dry lips, eyes bright.

'Two of my Police are outside,' continued his tormentor. 'Try anything and I'll scream and they'll be in here before you can twitch your whiskers. Except you can't, of course. Now listen, this is what I want. I want a flying child. You get

everywhere and you know everyone. I'm sure there's one somewhere. Maybe more. Find me one and bring it to me.'

'You want me to take a child from its family? What are you going to do with it?'

'I need a flying child for the magic show we're arranging. It would make a nice finale, don't you think?'

She crossed the room swiftly, flung open the stove and held the stone cat over the flames.

'It doesn't burn,' said Nathaniel hoarsely.

'Most things do in the end,' said Elfina. 'Or they can be crushed. Or lost at the bottom of the river. Come on, Nathaniel, cats aren't really like people. You don't care that much, do you? You look after yourself. Think of the long nights with the moon calling and the wind and the bright fresh smell of the river and you stuck in here clumsy and human with your eyes clouding and your knees aching. Think of it, Nathaniel. All finished. All gone.'

He gazed at her. Seeing the end of his life.

'I always get what I want,' she said. 'One way or another.'

'I know of a child,' whispered Nathaniel.

'Then get it.'

She was at the door and crossing the shop. He could see Mr Six and Mr Eight outside the window. She slammed the shop door and the ring of the bell echoed tiny and terrible in the silence she left behind.

Nathaniel and Elfina

After a while Nathaniel started to move stiffly around his room. He settled to sleep at last on his rocking-chair, which he found very uncomfortable in his human form. He jumped with a cry as the midday sun streaked the carpet around his feet. His eyes were staring and still dreaming he shouted in terror, 'Otto! Behind you! Run! Run! Run!'

Skull

Otto had been asleep all afternoon. Now he had woken up and Dolores had cooked him a big meal. He wanted to talk but she wouldn't let him.

'Just finish that bit,' she said, sitting next to him at the table, 'and have another of these.'

'I met some people who think Dad escaped at the library and I think he was the person that Madame Honeybun saw with FireBox,' he said desperately with his mouth full, as Dolores waved a second piece of something in his face.

'That is an interesting suggestion,' replied Morgan. 'Do you remember that he was here one evening, before that woman came on the television for the first time. FireBox had a piece of coal blocking a flame gland. Albert examined him and got it out and so forth. Dragons are very serious when it comes to things like that, they will always try to help someone who has helped them. And, of course, your father always got on very well with creatures. He has a connection with them.'

'I know nothing about that part of his life,' said Dolores, stonily. 'He kept everything a secret from me. And don't go talking to strangers, Otto.'

Madame Morgan sighed deeply. 'It has been very hard for the Karmidee people. There is no simple way for us to live our lives,' she said, 'even love can be difficult sometimes.'

At the mention of the word love, Dolores narrowed her eyes. 'He deceived me,' she said softly, 'he deceived us all.'

There was an uneasy pause.

'That woman was on the television again while you were cooking,' said Morgan. 'She's talking about butterflies now. It is her wish that they should all become extinct. Every last one. Anyone taking a sack of butterflies to the Town Hall will be given free tram travel for one year. They are all going on the Impossible List. The Midsummer Butterfly Festival is to be cancelled. Ever since I was a little girl I've loved watching them on Midsummer's Eve, flying down from BlueRemembered and TumbleMan, searching for their true loves. They mate for life, you know, they always find each other again.'

'Not this time,' said Dolores.

* * *

Otto was determined to start telling them all about the arena and Araminta's Gates. Then Pinfracca and Shinnabac came in from the garden, followed by Granny Culpepper smiling at everyone, and he jumped from his chair to slam the door shut.

'It's all right, Ottie, Madame le Grey and Pinfracca very kindly put a spell on the doorway to stop the twins flying out,' explained Dolores.

'Pinwackie,' said Zeborah, hovering to dip her toes in Otto's bowl of rice pudding.

'Aren't they sweet,' cooed Granny Culpepper.

'We've been discussing the situation,' said Dolores to Otto, 'and we think we should open the envelope Dad gave you to look after.'

Otto had felt calm enough to eat and, he had hoped, to talk. Now he felt bad again and he put down his spoon.

Morgan and Dolores both looked at him, waiting for him to say something. Meanwhile Zeborah sat down in his pudding.

'No,' said Otto.

'We might learn something from it, we might be able to show it to someone who can use it in some way. It might be some ancient spell or something. Al might not know what it is himself, and personally I think all this business about him having this mark and being a King could be a confusion—'

Skull

'No,' said Otto. Albert had told him to keep the envelope in his clothes and not take it out. Not even when he slept.

'He said he'd find a way to contact me,' he said solidly, 'and then he'll tell us what he wants. I'm to keep this in my clothes until then.'

'But, Ottie, he might not have meant—'

'That's what he SAID, Mum. And that's what I'm going to do because that's what he SAID.'

'Albert's no fool,' said Granny Culpepper in the quiet that followed. 'He'll come up with something.'

Dolores and Morgan said nothing.

'He told me not to take it out of my clothes and *he is the King of the Karmidee*,' said Otto. 'And I don't think I'll have this rice pudding now thanks.'

He decided to say no more.

At that moment, on the roof of the Town Hall, Albert was waking from a restless sleep with his head on FireBox's scaly neck.

As the street-lights came on and the Town Hall clocks struck nine, FireBox took off and Albert, clinging on to his back, raised a small bone whistle to his lips and blew a single piercing note into the spreading night.

The twins were finally asleep and Granny Culpepper, Morgan

and Dolores were discussing cats in the sitting room.

Otto sat at the kitchen window, looking into the shady little garden. Thinking about bandages. Injured legs. Counting the meals Albert hadn't had by now.

Something caught his eye on the wall. Another cat? Nathaniel Git himself? Half-man, half-cat and all mouth?

NO.

A big wolf jumped down on to the grass. He stood very still and looked at the house.

Otto had never seen a wolf so close. Normally they stayed on the mountains. Or down by the mud towns, some people said.

The wolf had very pale blue eyes full of moonlight. He found Otto's face at the window and after a moment he walked to the kitchen door.

With one paw he pushed it open.

Then he stopped again, silver and grey, very still, very real. There were dark marks on his face around his eyes that reminded Otto of a skull.

'. . . *your father is good with animals, especially our sort. Wild ones and Impossible ones . . .*'

Amos had said that.

The wolf inclined his head to one side. The way dogs do sometimes.

This was it then. It had to be.

Otto ran into the sitting room.

'Dad's sent someone to take me to where he's hiding,' he announced. 'Please can I take some food and is there such a thing as a portable crystal communicator? I want to take him one of those as well.'

'What do you mean Dad's sent someone, where are they?'

'In the garden, I've got to go now.'

Morgan, Dolores and Granny Culpepper all looked out of the window.

'That's not a person,' said Dolores, in horror. 'Don't let it in, Otto, bolt the door.'

But Morgan le Grey went quickly to the kitchen and came back with a canvas bag, wrapping some bread and other things in a cloth.

'Go to the dresser, Otto,' she said briskly, 'you'll find a little crystal communicator in the top drawer on the left.'

'My son is not going off into the dark with a WOLF,' shouted Dolores. 'I didn't look after him all these years to let him—'

'It's all right, Dolores,' said Granny Culpepper. 'The wolves are often the friends of the Karmidee.'

'Oh, for goodness' sake, Mother! Stop interfering! You used to be bad enough when you were Respectable! Now you're Impossible you're impossible!'

'That's Skull,' said Morgan le Grey calmly. 'I think Otto

must be right, I think your husband must have sent him.'

'BYE BYE,' said Otto.

As he stepped out of the kitchen door he heard his mother crying and yelling at the same time, 'Why didn't you tell me who I was? I don't know who I am! I'm not one thing or the other . . .'

He swung the bag onto his shoulder. It contained the food, the small crystal communicator and his tightly-rolled mat.

'Honourable greetings,' whispered Otto to the wolf.

They crept out of the door in the garden wall. Halos of misty rain hung around the street lamps.

Skull kept up a steady pace close to the shop fronts and Otto walked quickly alongside.

'Six eights are forty-eight,' he thought, the numbers bouncing through his head in time with his footsteps. He reached out and cautiously touched the thick fur on the back of Skull's neck. Then, since the wolf didn't seem to mind, he took hold.

The narrow streets were unusually busy.

They came to a small square where people seemed to have set up an unofficial market. There were sparse displays of jewellery and other valuables laid out under umbrellas and makeshift cardboard shelters.

Otto tried not to look anyone in the eye.

Skull

'The mines are never going to open again now,' he heard someone saying. 'I'm going to raise everything I can and then go and try my luck over on the muds. They're going to pull down all the stilt houses so they say, going to build some proper buildings. Magicos are all being moved out.'

'Good thing too,' said someone else. 'If it wasn't for them we'd still have our jobs.'

These people were moonstone miners then.

Out of nowhere a group of children surrounded Otto and Skull. They were all bigger than Otto.

'What's the hurry? What's in your bag?'

Otto tried to move forward but they stood in his way. He could feel Skull's hackles rising. The wolf's whole body seemed to be tightening under his fur.

'Come over here!' shouted one of them to someone across the square. 'I think we've got ourselves a little magico, smells like one, dresses like one, let's see if he's got any tattoos—'

'If he'd just open his mouth we'd all know. Should we have a little chat about fruit, what is there, apples, oranges, and what are those yellow ones called?'

'Watch out for that dog,' warned a girl, who was ignored.

If he spoke they would know him at once for a citizen. But he didn't speak.

Then there was a thud of footsteps.

'Let's see—' said a voice and the little crowd parted.

Otto and the Flying Twins

A tall boy dressed in a torn leather coat. He looked younger than some of the others – but that didn't seem to matter, he was their leader.

He stopped when he saw Otto.

They looked at one another.

Everyone was waiting.

Then the boy reached out and pushed Otto's big patched hat a little bit further back on his head.

'That's better,' he said, very quietly. 'Style.'

'What's going on?' asked one of the others.

'Show me what's in the bag,' commanded the boy.

Otto held it out.

Skull growled softly.

The boy held the bag close to his face and looked inside. It contained bread and cheese for Albert, the flying carpet and the crystal ball. Even if a citizen didn't know exactly what the last two were they were enough to give Otto away.

'Just papers and stuff,' said the boy, handing it back. 'No food, nothing worth anything. Leave him.'

'But what about his clothes, Dan? You're not saying just let him go?'

'I'm saying leave him.'

'What? Have you gone crazy? He's a scummy little magico runt—'

Skull

'I SAID LEAVE HIM. Or do you want to make the decisions round here these days, Si?'

The boy called Si hesitated.

'Let's sort it out now,' whispered Dante.

No one spoke.

Si looked away and some of the others laughed nervously.

Skull began to walk slowly forwards and, silent again, they stepped out of his way.

Then the wolf stopped and looked up at Otto and knocked against his leg and Otto, guessing, jumped on to his back. There was a terrifying snarl and with one great bound they were off.

Otto looked back over his shoulder for a last glimpse of the boy in the torn leather coat. Too late.

They were diving across the square and on up street after street after street into a part of HighNoon Otto had never seen before, even stranger and older than the rest.

THE KING OF THE *Karmidee*

They had come to a dead-end street with a boarded-up building at the bottom.

The entrance had once been lit by lamps on curling brackets. The doors had perhaps been rather splendid, with a flight of curved steps down to the pavement. Over these doors, very faded and peeling, Otto could see some sort of a sign. Too dark to try and work out what it said.

A creaking sound came from above. The wind?

The creaking grew louder. The air seemed to be coming to life over the rooftops. Skull growled and they both looked up and there was FireBox lumbering down out of the sky, clawed feet outstretched. Steam and flames hissed and flared around his mouth, his great leathery wings rattled, his spiked tail slammed into a lamppost as he landed, wild-eyed, on the littered pavement.

Albert was clinging on to his back.

'Dad!' yelled Otto, above the noise and heat.

'Stay where you are!' yelled Albert.

FireBox gave a great roar of triumph, scorching the nearest wall and some of the pavement and covering everything with ash. He sank down and gave the lamppost one last swipe with his tail. Albert dismounted.

'Dad!'

'Sssh!' Albert put his finger to his lips. Pointless really, given all the noise FireBox had just made.

'We've got to get in here.'

'Where?'

'Here.'

Albert was poking at the padlock on the chain which held the two doors together. He had a nail and was trying to spring it open.

'I thought you'd been arrested. Then I heard you'd got away.'

'Albert the Librarian doesn't get arrested. Help me with this.'

They fiddled for a little while longer. Even if they had any idea what they were doing, which they hadn't, it was pointless because the lock was jammed through with rust.

Then FireBox stood up and hooked one purple claw behind the padlock and it came away, bringing with it the door handles.

'Thank you, friend,' said Albert.

FireBox breathed a cloud of smoke and everyone coughed.

'No!' cried Albert, as the dragon squared himself up to ram the doors open with his huge shoulder.

'Thank you, thank you!' yelled Albert. 'We can open them now. We want them to close again afterwards,' and he added in a whisper to Otto, 'all heart and muscle power, bless him.'

He pushed gently on the doors and they swung open.

'Skull, if you would be so kind as to accompany Otto . . .'

Skull pushed through the crack between the open doors.

'Go on, Ottie.'

'You are coming, aren't you?'

'Of course I'm coming. I just need to tell FireBox what we're doing, hurry up.'

Otto followed Skull and found himself in total darkness.

There was a groaning of hinges behind them, and then outside the unmistakable rattle of wings as FireBox prepared for take-off.

'Go straight ahead,' said Albert's voice.

They went straight ahead. Through doors and along passage-ways. Skull at the front making small sounds which seemed to indicate that he thought the whole expedition unwise.

'There should be a door to the left about here,' said Albert. 'Be careful, there's some curtains, might be a bit dusty.'

Otto floundered into a wall of velvet. It felt like a giant hand closing round him.

Suddenly the lights came on.

'Welcome,' said Albert, coming from behind a pile of strange-looking wooden bushes, 'to the Pearly Oak PlayHouse. The theatre of the Karmidee, closed by the Town Hall thirty years ago. Reopening under new management very soon. How's Mum and the twins?'

Otto fought his way out of the curtain.

'They're OK. Granny Culpepper turned into a unicorn for a while. She's a widge.'

Albert nodded. He had of course heard this from Nathaniel Crane.

'Here's your envelope, Dad. I've looked after it.'

'Good,' said Albert, taking it, 'I knew you wouldn't let me down.'

'I've got you some food and a crystal communicator and how is your leg, is it hurt?'

There was a piece of cloth bound around Albert's leg just below the knee. One of his shirt sleeves, in fact.

'I cut it on some glass when FireBox got me out of the library. What sort of food?'

They sat on the floor while Albert ate bread and bananas out of the canvas bag.

Otto had realized that they were on the stage. Two enormous curtains, suspended from somewhere lost in the dark above, separated them from the place where the audience would sit.

'Now,' said Albert, brushing crumbs off himself and onto the dusty floorboards, 'I want to tell you about this picture.'

He opened the envelope and took out a number of documents. Upside down on one Otto read, 'Pearly Oak PlayHouse, Autumn Programme.' It looked very old.

'I found that in the library,' said Albert. 'That's why I chose this place. Tell you in a minute. Now, there are a certain kind of Karmidee, very rare nowadays, called dammerung. They can change from a person into an animal and back again. Always the same animal.'

'Like a cat?'

'Yes. Dammerung comes from a word for twilight. They're not totally one creature or the other, you see. Twilight is the time when the night meets the day. It's not quite night and it's not quite day. Well, the dammerung are like that, they're sort of in between. They can live for a very long time too. Sometimes hundreds of years, as long as they can change into their animal form whenever they want.'

'Is Nathaniel Crane a damn-whatsit?'

'Yes, he is, although it's impolite to talk about it.'

'We met him, I didn't like him.'

'Well anyway, the point is that they're not so locked in time and place as the rest of us. Sometimes they see pictures of the future, maybe several possible futures. Sometimes it's just a glimpse. Sometimes it's a lot more complicated. Often about people they don't know, places they don't know, confusing and scary. They call it a farsight and they hate it.'

'Did Nathaniel Crane tell you all this, Dad?'

'No, certainly not. I just know it through being brought up in TigerHouse.'

'And it's got something to do with the envelope?'

'Yes.' Albert held up a piece of paper covered with drawings. 'This was found buried a long time ago. It was a custom of theirs. If they had one of their visions, a farsight, they drew what they had seen on something and buried it in among the roots of a tree. Which is exactly where this was found.'

'They just buried it?'

'Yes. You see they believed, and still do, the ones that are left I expect, they believe that trees are extremely important. Trees don't move from one place to another. Trees are rooted in the ground. They grow at the same steady pace. Spring, summer, autumn and winter. Nothing hurries them. Like

clocks. When the City was first built there were a lot of dammerung here. That's why it's so full of trees. They planted them.'

'So is this something about the future?'

'Hang on, I want to tell you about how it was found.'

Otto couldn't remember when Albert had ever talked this much all at once.

'You see Elfina found it. I was there too.'

'ELFINA!'

'Yes. We were friends. Or we had been.'

'FRIENDS!'

'Yes. She lived on a barge in Red Moon. Her father was a citizen, a really nasty piece of work. Her mother ran off. She was a magico.'

Not for the first time Otto felt the world tilt under his feet.

'So Elfina is part magico.'

'Yes.'

'So why does she hate them, us, why does she hate magicos so much?'

'That's probably why. She hated her mother for leaving her. It was a terrible thing to do. She was only six. Her father was a very bitter cruel man who spent most of his time dazed-out.'

'Why didn't you want to be a magico, Dad?'

'That's different, Otto, it wasn't that I didn't want to be a magico. I wanted to work with books and preserve Karmidee documents. The library was the only place. Remember when she turned up there?'

Otto did a Mab eye-roll. How could he forget.

'Yes, well, the point is she's been looking for this and for me, in fact, down in the mud towns for quite a while. She never thought of the library because she never thought I'd manage to get a job like that. But I did and I took the farsight with me because it needed to be kept in the right sort of conditions or it would disintegrate.'

'Looks OK to me,' said Otto.

'This is a copy. I made it because I realized when all this started that she would come looking for it eventually, and looking for me, and I would have to go into hiding.'

'But why does she want this so much?'

'If the Karmidee find something like this they try not to look, they bury it again at once. Giving it back to the tree to look after, you see, everything in its own time. Once she'd seen it, it was too late.'

Otto looked at the picture. A strange collection of drawings with writing, not much of it, tangled in here and there. There was a woman at the top, holding what looked like a miniature version of the City in her hands. She seemed to be standing on a pile of money. Her clothes were decorated with numbers.

'She wants to make it come true, Otto. She wants to be that woman. Standing on a great pile of money and well, owning the City by the look of it.'

Otto stared. The numbers on her clothes seemed familiar.

'This writing here, can you see it, it's in the old language of the Karmidee. Here, it says,

> "She will become the richest citizen who has ever lived. But at great cost. To do it she must forget a part of herself. And what will happen if we deny ourselves? If we forget the beginning? If the enemy we despise is really in our hearts?" '

They both looked at the page for a moment.

'And here,' continued Albert, 'these things here, see, I think this tells us another future. In this future she can be stopped. But then it's like a riddle,

> "We must all be joined again at the same place and at the same time. That which was one and became two becomes one again."

There are these two halves of a tree. Two butterflies. Two striped cats and this heart in two. Whatever they are they all have to come together again.'

'And she knows you've got this, Dad, and you might work out the answer?'

'She knows it's a race to work it out.'

'So she's after you for two reasons then, because of this and because you are the King.'

Albert nodded.

Skull, who had fallen asleep, reached his paws along the floor in a dream of his own. Albert stood up and beckoned Otto into the shadowy wings. They made their way round the side of the big curtains and came out at the front of the stage. Otto could see the whole theatre now with its great domed roof, galleries and boxes and row upon row of dusty seats.

'The curtains,' said Albert.

Otto looked. It was hard to see at first because he was so near and the curtains were so dusty themselves. Then he recognized the Pearly Oak, embroidered on the velvet, just as it was in the picture, half on one curtain and half on the other.

'The two halves of the tree,' said Albert. 'There's a picture of the stage in that programme you were looking after. We can open and close them. One becomes two becomes one. This place was closed before she was born, I bet she doesn't know about it.'

The theatre seemed very big and silent all around them.

'The Karmidee despise me, Ottie,' said Albert. 'As far as

they're concerned, Araminta was the only one who was any use. They still talk about her. But maybe, with this, I can help them after all.'

'They don't all despise you, Dad,' exclaimed Otto. 'I've got a friend called Mab, with a mat, a flying one, and she's got two friends called Amos and Lydia, they believe in you.'

Albert smiled.

'We went to the Whispering Park,' said Otto quickly, 'and I was 360.'

Albert raised his eyebrows and smiled a bit more.

'Were you indeed.'

'Yes, but it must be wrong because I can't do anything. I can't fly like the twins, or make colours, or call animals . . .'

'Wait and see,' said Albert. 'Skull trusted you. He's only ever trusted me before.'

'Really?'

'Really.'

Otto grabbed the last bit of bread and crammed it into his mouth.

Then he recounted everything. Red Moon, the arena, the mats, the wind, and the men clearing the road on the other side.

'. . . and she's getting everyone to kill butterflies,' he added. 'She was on TV.'

'If she's clearing the road then she's going to try and reopen the Gates,' whispered Albert. 'She's going to bring Outsiders in to see these shows, and see the rest of the City too. It's full of totally Impossible things. Like nothing they've ever seen. The only thing is she's got to unlock all the spells on the Gates first. Fetch that crystal ball thing you brought with you. We must warn the people at once. And we must find Araminta before Elfina does.'

'Find her? I thought she lived hundreds of years ago.'

'Three hundred. But that's not the point. After the Gates were built she announced that she wanted to rest. She disappeared and others were born with the mark. But Araminta was a dammerung.'

Talking to the Launderette

'Calling the FireBox Launderette, calling the . . .'

'Wash your cares away', it said inside the communicator in spiky letters. Then the sign disappeared and there was Granny Culpepper wearing a little green hat with a daisy on.

'Albert!' she cried, clapping her hands, 'I'll get Dolores for you, Albert, they're all in the garden, Mr Crane has brought a cat for Dolores to meet—'

'Dad's safe,' interrupted Otto.

'I need you all to come to this thing and listen,' said Albert, with unusual firmness. 'Tell Dolores to make Mr Crane go away. I don't want anyone else to hear this.'

'Tell him where to go,' added Otto helpfully.

Granny Culpepper nodded and went out of the picture. A

small hand appeared from above, palm pressed on to the glass. Sounds of giggling.

Muffled voices could be heard, growing nearer.

Then Dolores, Morgan le Grey and Granny Culpepper all arrived at once, crowding their faces together.

'Honourable greetings,' said Albert.

'Is Ottie all right?' asked Dolores coldly.

'Yes, Mum, Dad's got a plan.'

'Are you alone now? Has Mr Crane gone?'

'Just left,' said Morgan.

'As King of the Karmidee I am asking you to keep what I have to say secret for the present time.'

'An honourable request which I will respect,' said Morgan.

'Me too,' said Granny Culpepper.

'You're the one who's good at keeping secrets, Al,' said Dolores.

'It's important, Mum,' said Otto. Even in the middle of everything he noticed how horrible and tiring it was that his parents weren't friends any more.

'Elfina is a magico, she's a sleeper, she's planning to get rich by bringing Outsiders in to see the City and watch the magic shows. She's just using the Impossible List to help her catch magicos. All the *really* Impossible things are being kept as they are – for Outsiders to come and see.'

There was shocked silence inside the crystal communicator.

'Look at it this way,' added Albert. 'She's selling us all, even the citizens.'

'Outsiders. Here,' whispered Madame Morgan. 'It will be the finish of us.'

'Do you remember the stories they used to tell us when we were children?' said Granny Culpepper, solemn at last. 'About people from their armies who thought widges and their cats could be used as weapons?'

Somewhere behind the three faces there was a huge crash.

Morgan and Granny Culpepper rushed out of sight.

Dolores stayed. Her face still. Amber eyes, amber skin. Like a painting, framed in the crystal.

'It's good to see you,' said Albert after a moment.

'Make sure nothing happens to Otto,' she said, as if this was all there was to say.

'Dad hurt his leg,' said Otto.

Morgan le Grey was back.

'FireBox has just landed in the garden,' she announced. 'Only one tree broken.'

'I want to hold a concert tomorrow evening in the old PlayHouse, the Pearly Oak,' said Albert. 'We'll advertise it, get lots of citizens in, and magicos too if we can. There's a jazz band who'll help us, they're citizens, but musicians don't care whether people are magico or not. Dolores, you'll have to organize the dancers. Then I'll talk to the audience. Tell them what's really happening. Everyone must know. That's the first thing.'

'Are you used to public speaking?' asked Morgan le Grey.

'Dad can do it,' said Otto.

Albert and Morgan began making plans for the concert. All of them, including Morgan, were to move over to the PlayHouse that night.

'There's more,' said Albert, 'Otto is going to help me. We need to speak to Grandpa Culpepper.'

'What about?' snapped Dolores. 'He's in danger already because of you. Mother crept out, although I told her not to, and phoned him. He told her that the Normal Police have been round to their house asking about you and he's going into hiding. He said she'd know where he meant.'

'Where?'

Granny Culpepper reappeared holding Zebbie. 'I think he means Guido's Beach.'

'I don't want my father sleeping on a beach!' exclaimed Dolores. 'He should be safely out playing golf somewhere. I don't want him involved in any of this.'

The whole picture turned white.

Something was dripping down it from above.

'Oh, the rice pudding,' trilled Granny Culpepper's voice, 'what a little moogbat you are, Zebbie.'

'Put it down!' That was Dolores yelling.

Too late it seemed.

The picture, what was left of it, tipped sideways, flickered and went black.

Guido's Beach

Otto flew down low over the groves of glowing lantern trees that separate Guido's Beach from the City. Beyond them he saw the beach itself. The air was very warm, there were palms bending in a pleasant breeze and moonlight sparkled on the river which, inexplicably, was lapping on the sand with the rhythm of a gentle sea.

He landed the carpet beside a row of beach huts.

Immediately a tall young man appeared from somewhere. He was barefoot and had long hair and when he spoke it was in the accent of the mud towns. Guido himself.

'Can I help you?' he asked, as if Otto had walked into a shop.

'I'm looking for someone,' said Otto. He knew the beach

was a well-known refuge for the magicos, although he couldn't see anywhere to hide.

'Aren't we all,' said Guido, cheerfully, 'we're all looking for someone. Or something. Fruit for example, those yellow ones that taste like a wasp spat on your tongue.'

'I know I *sound* as if I am very Normal,' said Otto, clinging on to his mat. 'I come from Parry Street. But my mother has just recently found out that her mother is a widge. And my father is really a magico. And my grandfather is supposed to be here somewhere and I've got to find him, it's very important—'

'No disrespect to you,' said Guido, 'but it's always very important. How do I know you're not working for the Normies?'

'Well I came here on this mat, didn't I?'

'It could be stolen. Are you a widge? Where's your cat?'

'My grandmother has a cat called Shinnabac. I went to the Whispering Park and I'm 360.'

'How did you know about the Park?'

'Mab took me there.' He pulled the matchbox out of his pocket and opened it. The beetle stirred sleepily in the moonlight. 'She gives me this beetle. When I need her I let it go and it flies off and finds her.'

'If you're 360 how does your energy manifest?'

Otto was feeling sicker and sicker. This was the worst

question yet. He wasn't even sure he understood it.

'I don't know,' he said simply. 'Nothing ever happens, but my sisters—' he stopped himself on the brink of the secret.

'Your sisters what?'

'Nothing,' said Otto.

Guido was looking at him carefully.

'Little Mab,' he said with a smile, 'little moth I call her. She's a tough one. Broke her arm last night, crashing into a tree. They took her away to the City Hospital. Confiscated her mat by all accounts.'

'WHERE?!' cried Otto, horrified. 'I must go and see her. She'll need help. I'll get her out of there. Tell me—'

'OK, OK that was an honourable way to speak. I'm sorry, I just had to test your story. She's fine as far as I know. Although she's been looking thinner every time I've seen her since her grandmother was arrested. She lives alone now. Not good for a little kid.'

'LIVES ALONE?'

'For months. There you are then, she's a proud one. Didn't tell you, I imagine. Very proud, our little moth. Her granny designed the Whispering Park, you know. Look, let's get to your grandfather. I've got more visitors coming.'

Otto looked up and saw a small party of people with a heavily laden donkey coming down to the beach through the trees.

'Follow me,' said Guido.

And Otto followed him, reeling in his head and still somehow finding time to be pleased that Guido had never once called him Mr Normal or pointed out that he was small.

'Where are we going?' he asked.

'Just here,' laughed Guido, opening the door to the nearest beach hut.

Otto followed him inside.

It was brightly lit and seemed not to be a hut at all. It was an entrance. They went down a deep flight of steps and the air became hotter and damper. Then there was a very long passageway which Otto judged must be leading back under the lantern trees. He began to hear voices and splashing and running water.

'Take your shoes off,' said Guido.

They had reached a pair of large wooden doors.

Otto took off his shoes. He tied them together by his laces and hung them around his neck.

'Good man,' said Guido. 'Mind you don't slip.'

He opened the doors and they entered an enormous room and there was a huge tiled swimming pool with elegant fountains, a spiral water chute, mosaics and statues. Blue and green children waved to them from the shallows and merpeople were basking on a little island in the middle.

'You didn't know about the Municipal Baths?' said Guido,

leading him around the edge to the other side. 'The cavers dug all this out at the beginning for their friends, the water people. The Normals have never found them. A lot of these people have come here in the last few weeks. Scared to stay in the river, especially the ones with webbed feet.'

Otto saw some little girls, much the same size as Hepzie and Zeb, playing in a sort of bubbly pool.

'I bring them food and everything,' Guido was explaining, 'I look after the underground. Here we are—'

They had come to some more doors and Otto put his shoes on. Then there were a lot more passageways with mysterious entrances leading off with things written over them like 'Mook Cave', 'Jacob's Sheep – Winter Stores', 'Parrot Maintenance'.

Finally they stopped outside one which said, 'Billiard Room'.

'Now, before we go in,' said Guido, lowering his voice and sounding serious, 'these cavers are very jumpy. They usually stay up in SmokeStack because that's the warmest mountain and they like it hot, but she sent Normies up there with lights and stuff and tricked some of them. They can't see in bright light, as you no doubt know, right?'

Otto nodded. He had no idea what Guido was talking about.

'Well she dazzled some of them in a tunnel and got them all chained up for her Digging Gang. A couple escaped and

they're here. The others are here because they think it's the only safe place at the moment. Now, your grandfather, he's quite a personality, seems to be able to get on with anyone, he's in here with them but be careful, all right, because they're tense. And, of course, they have been known to eat people when they're wound up and that would be a shame.'

And with these words Guido gave Otto an encouraging thump between the shoulder blades, opened the door and left him standing inside at the top of a flight of steps.

Otto gulped. He was looking down into a large dimly-lit room full of tables with fringed lamps hanging over them.

The air was hot and dry. The coloured billiard balls rolled and clacked.

It wasn't people playing at the tables.

Creatures Otto had never seen before moved slowly back and forth in the smoky light. They walked upright and wore studded waistcoats and they talked, it seemed, like people, except their voices were deep and scratchy.

Apart from that they were nothing like people at all. They were like very, very big lizards and as they bent to line up a shot they flicked their forked tongues over their dusty lips.

Otto looked around for his grandfather.

There he was halfway across the room. It looked as if the game was nearly over.

Otto set out, creeping between the tables, glad to be small.

A caver turned and knocked into him and then, seeing him, stood in his path. He looked as old and tough as the mountains.

Otto didn't dare speak. He bowed and removed his large magico hat.

To his relief, the caver bowed in return. He was chewing bloodberry leaves and his mouth was stained red with juice. At least Otto hoped it was bloodberry juice.

Grandpa Culpepper had seen him and was in conversation with his opponent.

As Otto arrived at their table he heard the caver saying, 'Well played, Isidor.'

'Ah, but you won in the end, Megrafix, and look, here is my grandson, what a pleasant surprise. And what a big hat. Allow me to introduce you, Megrafix, this is Otto. Otto, this is my friend Megrafix, an ancestor and a hero, recently escaped from the infamous Digging Gang.'

Otto bowed low once more. Megrafix nodded in return. Mention of the mysterious Digging Gang had made him sombre.

'There were five of us,' he said. 'First we were forced into the mines. Rock falls. Collapsing ceilings. Then we were driven into the drains. The drains! We who carved the mountain homes! Can you imagine our shame? Digging upwards then, up into the roads. Always the evil light in our

eyes. We, the cavers, the ancestors, scrabbling like rats through a pile of bones!'

Otto could not help shivering.

Then Megrafix took hold of one of the giant moonstones on his waistcoat with his clawed hand and pulled it free. He held it out to Otto.

'Your grandfather has told me who you are,' he said. 'Give this to your father. Tell him we will die for him.'

Otto stared up into his eyes and saw tears there.

'I will do so,' he replied.

Then Grandpa Culpepper and Otto took their leave.

Guido had wisely given Grandpa Culpepper a small guidebook.

'Guide to Passages and Underground: Simplified: South Quarter Only. Unsafe thoroughfares marked in Orange. Drinking fountains indicated by pictures of Little Taps.'

Grandpa Culpepper, despite his hasty departure from his home, looked as clean and well-dressed as ever. His suit was excellent grey summer-weight wool, his waistcoat a beautiful cream brocade, and his shoes, as always, were polished to perfection. He carried a small overnight bag with crate birds embroidered on the side.

He was leading the way and all was going well when they

rounded a corner – and there was a caver looking desperate and dirty and dangerous.

He grabbed Grandpa Culpepper by the collar and lifted him up with one hand.

'Who are you?' he croaked. 'I've just smashed my way out of these,' he held up a manacle dangling from his other wrist. 'I'm going to kill the first Normal I see.'

Grandpa Culpepper threw the map on to the stone floor. Otto grabbed it. All he knew was that they were making for a door marked 'Refreshments'. There it was just two doors down from where they were.

'I am a friend of Megrafix, hero and ancestor,' said Grandpa Culpepper with difficulty.

'Have you ever been hungry?' enquired the caver. 'Doesn't look like it to me,' and he prodded the brocade waistcoat, which was pleasantly curved. 'And if you're magico where are your tattoos?'

'I can't show you unless you put me down.'

Otto had found the door. He opened it. His grandfather was waving at him behind his back. Well, if he expected Otto to go without him he was wrong.

Grandpa Culpepper was now safely on the floor, rolling up his sleeve.

'And don't you move, either,' said the caver to Otto.

'Here,' said Grandpa Culpepper, baring his forearm, 'my

family symbols, two crate birds in flight.'

'I can't see anything,' said the caver suspiciously. Otto, who had crept nearer, knew there was nothing there.

'Well, they are very old,' sighed Grandpa Culpepper, 'and my skin is extremely dark—'

'All you humanoids look alike to me,' interrupted the caver, 'no scales, weird—'

'. . . except here,' persisted Grandpa Culpepper, turning his hand over to show the palm, 'which is pink, a delicate contrast which I inherited from my father.'

With the same hand, and gracefully, he slipped his gold fob watch out of his waistcoat pocket. 'And now we have to get on our way,' he said gently, 'and I would like you to have this, because you have suffered much and are in need.'

The caver took the watch. His hands were amazing, covered in scales that looked as hard as rock.

'I don't want your stuff,' he said quietly. 'I'm not a thief.'

'You're not stealing it,' said Grandpa Culpepper. 'It is a gift. Megrafix told me what you have all been through.'

He walked backwards towards the open door, Otto stumbling next to him.

The caver watched them go, blinking his weary eyes.

Madame Honeybun's

It was a spiral staircase and it went on for a very long time. At last, much out of breath, Grandpa Culpepper stuck his head through the trap door at the top. A cloud of good smells reached Otto, a few steps behind.

Familiar good smells.

'Honourable greetings,' said a warm voice. It was Madame Honeybun Nicely and this was the Amazing Cake Shop.

Madame Honeybun had her golden hair all piled on her head and she was wearing a deep blue satin dressing gown. She looked even more curvy than ever.

'My dear lady, I'm so sorry—' began Grandpa Culpepper.

'This trap door is a twenty-four hour facility,' she said firmly, 'and I am delighted to assist.'

Otto explained everything.

'But I know your grandmother Isabella well,' exclaimed Honeybun. 'We played together as children.'

Grandpa Culpepper smiled tenderly.

'Such a beauty when we met, and so strong and wild. But then, after Dolores was born you know, she wanted to be respectable. It didn't suit her. Made her somewhat tense.'

'She's a bit wild again now,' said Otto.

'Good, I'm looking forward to that. Be your true self, that's the secret.'

Easy if you know who that is, Otto replied in his head.

'And that's why I can be of help over this Araminta matter,' continued Grandpa Culpepper. 'To be quite honest, when we were young I had to rescue her from the police station on a number of occasions—'

'From the police station? Granny in the police station?'

'Indeed, there was the time she was trying out some new flying device or other and got stuck on the roof of the Town Hall, then there was the time she and that Shinnabac turned a tram into an elephant—'

'I remember that!' exclaimed Honeybun. 'It was in the papers and everything.'

'I took the precaution of obtaining my own set of keys and I've carried them with me ever since. This was before these

Normal Police we've got to put up with now, this was the old police station round the back of the Town Hall.'

'But how did you get keys, Grandad? I thought your job was to do with money.'

'I was Chief Accountant at the Town Hall by the time I chose to stop, Otto. But when your sweetheart could end up in prison at any moment, you find ways and means, I can assure you. I knew someone in the Maintenance Department and he had a great-grandmother who was a widge and he was most understanding. Anyway, I will draw you a plan and with the aid of your carpet and your friend Mab I think you can have a look in their records, they've got files there going back hundreds of years.'

THE Filing Cabinets

Otto and Mab were standing anxiously in the middle of a maze of filing cabinets, all of them twice as tall as they were. Mab had opened a window nearby in case they needed to leave in a hurry. They were in almost total darkness, the only light came from the moon at the window and Mab's eyes.

He fumbled with the map. Then he dropped it altogether for the third time.

'Get on with it,' she whispered. 'I bet you're still scared of flying as well.'

'I bet you're still living on your own.'

He heard her gasp with shock.

'I'm sorry,' he stammered immediately. 'Guido told me.

The Filing Cabinets

Why didn't you tell me? I thought we were friends. I keep finding out that people haven't told me stuff.'

Silence beside him in the dark.

'I would have got you food and things,' he said miserably.

'Just look for the one with A on,' she said. 'I'll help you because it's helping the King.'

As she swept her eyes up to the cabinet he caught a glimpse of the floor. It seemed to be covered in mosaic.

'Look down there,' he exclaimed, despite himself, 'even in here they've got crate birds and flowers and things all over the floor.'

She laughed, not the sort to join in with. 'You people really do think you invented this City, don't you? The Normals made this into a police station. It wasn't a police station before they came. The Karmidee don't have police.'

'What was it then?'

'Just another crazy, beautiful building. They just loved building things. Still would if they got the chance. Magical energy, makes it a lot easier, you wouldn't understand.'

'OK, OK, look, this is the one, look up there, light up that bit, the middle drawer.'

'You don't say please much, do you, Mr Normal?'

He waved the map in the air, banging his arm on a cabinet behind him, wanting to shout but managing a sort of screaming whisper. 'Look, I'm SORRY I said about you living

alone. I'm SORRY I'm different from you, I don't come from the muds and I don't talk like Amos and Lydia, but that's who I am. I'm ME. So don't call me MR NORMAL or MR SMALL, I am OTTO.'

That was it. He'd destroyed everything. The two beams of light faded. They wandered a moment over his face, then back to the cabinets. They had blurred as if they were shining through a mist.

'You don't understand,' she said softly, 'you've got a mum and a dad and a granny and a grandad and sisters and brothers or whatever and they all love you. And you've never got hungry. You don't even know what that feels like. You've got everything.'

'But . . .'

He stopped. Something was happening to him. He could still see the dark walls of cabinets and Mab, a shape in the shadows, her eyes no longer lit. But he could see something else as well, another scene, another room, very bare, a wooden floor, a cloth hanging over a doorway, and Mr Six and Mr Eight pushing a woman towards it. She had long grey hair, all tangled round her face, and she was struggling and writhing round to try and see someone over her shoulder.

It was Mab. A blanket clutched round her.

'Be proud, little moth,' cried the woman, 'we'll be together again.'

The Filing Cabinets

'Keep out of the way, kid,' said Mr Six, kicking at Mab as he and Mr Eight and the woman stumbled and fell through the curtain and the whole picture faded until only the cabinets and the dark were left.

Otto leant against the nearest cabinet. He could just make out Mab, exactly where she had been.

'*Be proud of yourself, little moth,*' he said, without thinking.

The two lights flared up like flames.

'What?'

'I just said, I just meant that you're right, I've never been hungry, you're right.'

They both fell silent.

'Is that the one we want?' said Mab. 'AR to CR?'

They pulled out the cumbersome drawer and found the file quickly.

It was thin and light and, like everything else in there, covered in dust. He opened it and Mab's eyes danced across the page inside.

There were only a few lines, written in elaborate curly writing, faded so much it was hard to read.

'Araminta Karmidee, date of birth unknown. Suspected of anti-citizen activities. Believed to be regarded by the magicos as some sort of leader although role unclear. Was thought to live alone in

Red Moon but may since have moved to the new
settlement nearby. No known relatives. Has not
been traced for some years.'

The date, at the end, was three hundred years old. In spidery
letters after it said,

'Case Closed.'

Otto replaced the page. That was it, then. He stretched up
to put the file back and as he did so, with Mab staring over his
shoulder, he saw something wedged in the bottom of the
drawer above.

'Look,' he whispered. It was another file. Perhaps it had
been left on top of the others and been caught up as the
drawer was closed.

'It could be anything,' hissed Mab.

'I'll just look. No. You get it.'

Before she had time to argue he picked her up round the
waist and lifted her. They staggered for a moment, hitting the
open drawer, then she made a grab for the file and pulled it
free.

'Quick,' said Mab, 'we've been here too long already.'

Otto was staring at the writing on the dusty cardboard.

'Quick,' she said again.

He pointed to the name on the outside and then he
opened it and tipped everything out. Something hard hit

the floor and skidded behind him somewhere. This time there were several pages of typed notes: it was a much more recent file.

The subject was Annalise Crink – convicted of forgery and theft. Height, tall. Brown hair, olive skin, distinctive birthmark on the back of the left hand. She had been arrested twenty-five years before. Her husband had written to the Mayor giving a list of all her crimes. His letter was in the file too. He had been the main witness at her trial, and her defence, that it was he who had committed the crimes, had obviously not been believed. She had lived with him on a barge in the mud towns and they had one child, a girl.

At the bottom there was a note added from the prison.

'A piece of jewellery, possibly stolen, was confiscated from the convict when she began her sentence and is enclosed in case it is claimed.'

'It's Elfina's mother,' whispered Otto. 'She didn't walk out, she was arrested.'

'Life imprisonment,' said Mab. 'She might still be in the prison now. What do you mean, she didn't walk out?'

'Tell you later, let's keep this. Hang on, there's more here—'

There was one page left. It was a letter from a prison guard, it seemed, to someone at the Town Hall called the Minister for Magico Control.

Dear Minister,

There is a rumour among the prisoners that Annalise Crink, serving life for several crimes, is actually one Aramincer, some sort of magico leader and a person of importance to them.

She denies this and continues to protest her innocence of her crimes. I thought perhaps this should be brought to your attention.

Yours with respect and admiration for your fine work,

The signature was all swirls.

Underneath someone else, presumably from the Ministry Office, had scrawled:

'One must assume that this imbecile is referring to Araminta, the legendary Queen of the Karmidee who is supposed to have lived about three hundred years ago. It would appear that the prisoners have been having some fun with him.'

The Filing Cabinets

There was a creak in the darkness and they both froze. From somewhere in the direction of the door there came the glow of a worm torch. Someone had come into the room very quietly. Someone else who didn't want to attract attention by putting on the lights.

Elfina

Otto started scuffling frantically around collecting the papers.
He pushed the file into Mab's hands as she ran to the window.
He was going to try and close the cabinet and run after her
but he stood on something that made him skid and fall. The
thing that had fallen out of the file. It was on a chain. He
picked it up and then shoved at the drawer, waving at Mab to
go, and mouthing PLAYHOUSE, PLAYHOUSE, and then he
heard someone behind him and then he was dazzled by a
horrible light, grabbed in powerful hands and pinned against
the opposite cabinets.

He kicked out and shouted, 'GO! GO!' This, of course,
was for Mab.

A voice spoke out of the light.

'I'm not going anywhere yet, little boy, and when I do leave you will be coming with me.'

At last she turned the beam away from his face. He still couldn't see her because his eyes were useless for a moment but he recognized her voice. It was Elfina.

She held on to his ear with a grip like a crusher and searched through the files in the open drawer.

He kicked again as hard as he could and sank his teeth into her wrist. Then he gasped in pain as she twisted his ear, not even bothering to look at him.

He craned around to see the window. To his horror Mab was just outside, hovering on her mat, her face bleached white by the moon.

He waved at her again to go.

'Keep still,' snapped Elfina, turning, Araminta's file in her hand. 'I know who you are, you're Albert's brat, aren't you? What a lucky find! You're going to be my hostage. He won't stand in my way while I've got you, will he?'

She read the entry in the file.

'Disappeared, without trace. Three hundred years ago. Araminta was the first sleeper! She ran away from her responsibilities. A common problem with you people.

'Your father sent you here for this, didn't he? Was he too scared to come himself? I got here just in time, it seems. You might have hidden it from me. Now I know there is no point

in scouring the place for her. There's another way to deal with the magic on those Gates, I'll get them open, don't you worry about that.'

Otto looked back at the window.

'No point in thinking about escaping,' sneered Elfina. 'You're leaving with me.'

Mab had gone.

BACK AT THE PlayHouse

Albert had cleared out some of the dressing rooms behind the stage for his family. They arrived after dark, disguised as a small party of sheep, an optical illusion provided by Madame Morgan and Pinfracca.

'Where's Ottie?' asked Dolores at once.

'He's gone to fetch something for me. I'm expecting him back very soon,' Albert had said. The unpleasant truth was that Otto was taking a long time.

Then Morgan had come from the doors of the theatre, followed by a skinny little magico girl who seemed to be very upset and trying to keep her dignity.

'This is Mab,' said Morgan. 'She and Ottie have been in the old police station. She has something for Albert. I'm sorry to

have to tell you that Otto is now a prisoner of Elfina.'

There was a hateful, painful silence.

Then, 'You useless fool,' whispered Dolores at Albert, 'you stupid useless two-faced murdering fool!'

Albert was trembling.

'Otto is not murdered,' said Morgan. 'Mab here heard Elfina tell him that she will hold him hostage to stop Albert from, as she put it, "getting in her way". And Mab has something to show to Albert herself, by herself, as she thinks this is what Otto will be wanting her to do.'

'Get Nathaniel Creep on the glass ball thing NOW,' said Dolores. 'I want to meet that cat he says he has found NOW, TONIGHT. Then I am going to get Ottie back myself. I'm a widge, aren't I? I'LL TURN THAT BITCH INTO A WORM AND STAMP HER INTO THE GROUND.'

Otto AND Elfina

Otto sat next to Elfina in her special Town Hall carriage with the steam-driven motor. Mr Six and Mr Eight were coming too.

'My flat,' commanded Elfina to the driver. And to Otto, 'Don't try to jump out or anything heroic. You might have an accident and we don't want to upset Daddy, do we?'

The doors were locked anyway. They drove slowly down the Boulevard where the cafés were still open and a man was selling the silvery balloons known as drifters. Otto saw a man and a woman buy one and then take hold of the string together and float a little way into the air. They glided gently along the pavement, smiling and talking. He suspected that this was Impossible but he wasn't completely sure.

Elfina lived in a very expensive building opposite the Winter Gardens. She had a flat on the top floor. They all went up in the lift and it was only then that Otto realized he had dropped his mat back at the old police station.

The windows of her lounge had been enlarged so that it seemed as if there was a wall of glass. On the other side of the Boulevard the snow-covered gardens twinkled in the moonlight. There were leather armchairs and stone tables. Mr Six and Mr Eight finally disappeared.

'My City,' she said with an elegant wave of her arm. 'Good view, don't you think?'

There on a table in the middle of the room lay the farsight, crumbling just as Albert had predicted it would do.

'Has your dear father worked all these things out yet? The tree split in two, that's Araminta's Gates. They're shut now. I'll get them open and I'll make sure they'll never shut again. I was going to make our heroine Araminta undo her magic, but since she can't be found I'm going to be using something from the Outside.

'And this heart in two, that's the mountain. BrokenHeart. It's in two right now, and it would take another earthquake to close that. I don't think there's much to worry about there.

'Then we've got these rather beautiful butterflies. The famous butterflies who live on the mountains and come down to be reunited with their lifelong loves each midsummer's eve. No problem there. All dead.

'And then there's these two, the stripy cats. I think that problem has just about been solved too, I was getting rid of cats anyway to stop any amplification, if you understand what I mean. It's amazing how low people will stoop for a reward. Mind you the economy has rather suffered since the mysterious rockfalls in the mines.'

Otto sat rigid. Her words were clawing at him.

The telephone rang.

'A concert!' exclaimed Elfina in a delighted voice. 'Tomorrow night! But that's so soon, Cedric, what short notice . . . oh, well if it's free we can't say no, can we . . . no I haven't heard of that theatre . . . or, wasn't there one called that a long time ago? . . . really, in HighNoon . . . very unusual . . . yes, of course I'll come, my sweetiepie . . . I'll have a guest, I'll bring him too, shall I? And I'm looking after the son of an old friend for a few days . . . I knew you wouldn't mind . . .'

She put down the phone.

'This is interesting, do you know anything about it? Sounds like a magico thing to me.'

'I doubt it,' said Otto painfully, 'the magicos are a bit distracted at the moment.'

Elfina wasn't taking any chances. She called Mr Six and Mr

Otto and the Flying Twins

Eight and instructed them to attend the concert with her and to arrest the organizers at the end.

Then she stood at the window and cracked her knuckles and then, for the first time, she left the room and he was alone.

The portable crystal communicator was in his pocket and he closed his hand around it.

She came back, carrying a tray with a coffee pot and two mugs and what looked like sandwiches.

'No point in letting you starve,' she said. 'You're only useful if you're alive.'

He had no intention of eating, his mouth felt alien and dry. Anyway, it might be a trick. A sedative. Or worse.

'Not hungry? No matter, I'll have yours.'

He had never seen anyone eat the way she did. It was very quick and although it was tidy too it seemed as if she was tearing at those sandwiches, as if her teeth were much sharper than other people's.

She licked her lips and yawned behind her hand.

'I don't sleep much,' she said. 'You lie down if you like on the sofa. The bathroom is just through there, by the way. There's no window.'

Sleeping, like eating, seemed dangerous. He stayed sitting up.

'As you like,' she said dryly and then she opened a desk by

the window and sat there for a while reading through papers, signing things and gazing out, from time to time, at the city which she had described as hers.

Otto tried to concentrate on staying awake.

'What do you think I should do with your father when I catch him?' she said suddenly, swinging round on her chair. 'A lot of Karmidee were executed in the old days, you know, or banished, sent to the Outside.'

He said nothing.

'You love him, don't you? And he loves you, to judge by the fuss he made at the library when Six and Eight tried to pick you up.

'That's all a mystery to me. Fathers, mothers, love, all that stuff.

'Like all that loyalty and honour business. Why are you so loyal to him, sitting there like a little rock? He's letting his people be sold like cattle. I should know. I'm the one doing the selling.'

'No, he isn't!' yelled Otto. 'He is the King of the Karmidee and . . .'

He had managed to stop himself.

'. . . and what, little boy?'

'Nothing. That's who he is, that's all.'

'I tell everyone a pack of lies about my childhood. The truth is my mother left us and my father hated me. That's why

it's easy for me to do what I'm going to do. I'll pocket the money and leave, just like my dear mother did. I've never loved anyone, you see, and no one has ever loved me, except his Mayorfulness of course, who is pathetic.'

Suddenly it happened to Otto again. Heartsight. He was looking at her and she began to disappear. The harsh room with the comfortless furniture was taken over by another scene.

He gripped the chair with his hands.

He was looking at a strange narrow room. There was a strong smell of the river. It was a barge. A woman, with long hair, was leaning over a little girl who was sitting down.

'You are my treasure,' said the woman, touching the little girl's face. 'You are my treasure and that makes me rich. Money comes, money goes, but love is love.'

The little girl was smiling.

Then they both seemed to hear something and turned their heads. And Otto was sure now who they must be.

It all faded, just like the picture of Mab and her grandmother.

'You are my treasure,' said Otto, *'and that makes me rich. Money comes, money goes but love is love.'*

'WHAT did you say?'

'It wasn't me that said it, it was someone else a long time ago when you were a little girl.'

'What are you talking about?'

He felt as if he was opening the cage of a dangerous animal. She was staring at him with her beautiful terrible eyes, as if she stared through bars.

'Your mother, she said it all, *you are my treasure*, she said that.'

Elfina jumped to her feet and swept the papers off her desk.

'MY MOTHER DUMPED ME, SHE LEFT ME,' she spat. 'AS FAR AS I'M CONCERNED SHE NEVER HAPPENED.'

'I'm just saying what she said,' said Otto stubbornly. 'Perhaps she didn't dump you, perhaps something happened that stopped her coming back.'

'Wait there!' shouted Elfina. 'I'm going to show you something!'

She thundered out of the room. Shaking he tried to get the communicator out of his pocket but she came back so quickly again that he didn't have time.

She flung off her coat, revealing an amazing silver and black dress, and then slammed a book in front of him on the table.

'This is how I'm going to open those stupid Gates!'

The book was called *The Invention of Gun Powder*.

'I can get some of this. It'll burst open like a firework, a much, much bigger firework and it'll blow a hole in those Gates bigger than a double-decker tram.'

But for Otto the barge, the lantern-lit room, the woman with her little girl were like a shield and a weapon against her.

He was scared that she would hit him but he spoke as clearly as he could.

'She said, *You are my treasure*,' he said, '*money comes, money goes, but love is love*.'

Elfina strode past him.

'Good night,' she whispered, 'you stupid little boy.'

Then she picked up the book and left the room in darkness.

Dolores AND Wishtacka

No one had slept at the Pearly Oak PlayHouse. Morgan le
Grey had summoned Nathaniel Crane who had brought a cat
for Dolores. Honeybun Nicely and Grandpa Culpepper had
arrived shortly afterwards on the red and gold traction engine
that she used for delivering cakes.

The widges were on the stage now, practising magic. The
cat was called Wishtacka.

'Now,' said Morgan patiently, 'let's try again, you have to
think the words of the spell and stare straight into Wishtacka's
eyes. She, in turn, stares at the object, in this case this piece of
cake. Are you ready, Wishtacka?'

Wishtacka gazed back at everybody. It certainly looked as
if she had emptied her brain.

Dolores had bound up her hair with several scarves from the costume department, one of which had little silver bells on. She was wearing a long purple dress with a silver sash, also from the costume department. She looked magnificent.

She stared at Wishtacka, both of them stern with concentration.

'Now!' said Morgan.

The cake trembled. Then, with terrifying speed it was covered in flames, then they were gone and the cake was still there. Except it looked different. It had turned to stone.

Dolores turned to Morgan with a look of triumph.

'I have never seen anyone learn such a difficult spell so fast,' said Morgan. 'Honourable congratulations. It wears off after a time but under the circumstances I would suggest that no one eats that cake.'

'Now I'm going to find Ottie,' said Dolores.

Honeybun and Morgan had spent much of the night stopping Albert and Granny Culpepper from rushing out with the same purpose.

'You have no idea where he is and you will be arrested before you get out of HighNoon,' said Honeybun.

'Just let anyone try to arrest me,' replied Dolores, who was definitely no longer totally respectable.

'Elfina needs Otto as a hostage. She will make herself known,' said Morgan firmly, 'then something can be done.'

Dolores and Wishtacka

Dolores picked up Wishtacka and held her close to her face and the others found themselves confronted by two pairs of ruthless eyes.

'Something's going to be done all right,' said Dolores.

Granny Culpepper and Mab were looking after the twins. Mab had been given some sort of special cake by Madame Nicely called a Raspberry Reviver, she was to take small bites and chew carefully.

Meanwhile Nathaniel Crane had stayed on after the cat deal had been completed. Zebbie was standing on his head.

'Have you a fever, Mr Crane?' asked Granny Culpepper. 'You look so pale and you keep shaking, you would be better at home, wouldn't you? And we don't want anyone seeing you leave in daylight, you might give us all away.'

'Don't worry about me, Madame,' he laughed. 'Nobody sees Nathaniel if he doesn't want to be seen.'

But he was speaking of his other form. The part of him that was lost. He closed his hands around Zebbie's ankles.

Albert and Grandpa Culpepper came out from the dressing room where they had been talking and everyone except Dolores looked at them expectantly.

'We're going to get Elfina's mother out of the prison,' said Albert. 'We think she is Araminta.'

Just then the crystal communicator lit up.

'Otto!' cried Albert and Dolores.

And there was Otto, in some terrible dark room with frightening furniture.

Dolores snatched the crystal away from Albert.

'Ottie! Are you all right? Where are you?'

'In the flat,' whispered Otto, 'I'm in her flat, listen Dad, she's coming to the concert. She's going to arrest people. She's going to bring me too. And the Mayor—'

'We'll get you back,' said Albert.

'I will,' said Dolores.

'And Dad, there's something else, about the Gates—'

The picture was suddenly flooded with light.

Otto turned away, they could see his fingers close over the screen as he tried to pick it up. Everything blurred. Then there was a wail of horror in the PlayHouse. Otto's face had gone. It was Elfina looking at them now.

'I see you, Albert Karmidee,' she said, 'I see you and I've got your little beloved here. If you want to see him again come to the concert at the Pearly Oak PlayHouse tomorrow night. I'll swop. You for him.'

'Wishtacka!' commanded Dolores.

'You can't do anything over the air,' said Morgan hurriedly, 'has to be face to face, I'm afraid.'

'Goodnight, everyone,' said Elfina, 'sweet dreams.'

The communicator went dark.

Dolores and Wishtacka

They all stared into it for a few moments longer.

'Go and get Araminta if you want,' said Dolores to Albert without looking at him. 'Do what you like. But this farsight thing is all rubbish. Get Araminta, catch two butterflies, find two cats, whatever you like, but make sure you are back for the concert to give yourself up. At least you can do that for your son.'

THE CARVED
Stone Cat

'What exactly is this?' demanded Elfina.

'It's a crystal communicator,' said Otto.

'How does it work?'

'I don't know. You just talk into it.'

He wasn't exactly giving anything away by saying that.

She was holding it in her long fingers, turning it round.

'Interesting,' she said.

'Lots of magico things are interesting,' said Otto, reckless with exhaustion. 'This is something that widges use.'

'All for sale now,' she retorted and she locked it in her desk. 'Get some sleep. We're meeting an important visitor in the morning.'

* * *

The Carved Stone Cat

Alone in the barren room once more Otto lay down on the unfriendly sofa. After some thought he got up and picked up a rug. He was about to pull it over him when he realized that it was wolf-skin. Sick at heart he let it slide back to the floor.

Then he felt something warm against his chest. It was the jewellery thing from the file. Despite the fact that it was quite big and bumpy he had forgotten that he had put it around his neck.

He went over to the window, where the sky was beginning to grow light and held it up to look. It was a carved stone cat, made from that very hard very black stone that the miners sometimes found, called obsidian. There were moonstones on its paws and rubies in its eyes. And it was warm. Warmer than he was. Almost as if it was alive.

Mr Sleight

He was woken by a banging on the door of the flat. Elfina glided through the room on her way to open it. So she even had breakfast in her raincoat.

'Get up, little magico,' she said over her shoulder.

He was stiff all over and his head hurt. Today was the day that his family was going to be arrested.

'Be proud,' he thought to himself, hoping she'd got to the theatre safely.

Mr Six came in with a man wearing strange clothes and carrying a briefcase. He looked as if he had walked a long way out of doors. His trousers were marked and torn, his shoes looked terrible and he definitely needed a shave.

'Mr Sleight, come in,' said Elfina, all smiles. 'I trust you had a pleasant journey.'

He sat down heavily on a chair. Undoubtedly the answer was no.

'Mr Sleight has come from the Outside to see our lovely City, Otto,' said Elfina, still doing the smile. 'He has been travelling for days. Mr Six met him on the mountain and brought him through the tunnels. Mr Eight is bringing up his tent and his other bags now, I imagine.

'Let me get you a cup of coffee and some breakfast,' she added. 'Would you like a steak?'

'Just the coffee,' said Mr Sleight, rather faintly. He slowly unlocked his briefcase.

Otto peered at the mysterious contents. A black box with little buttons with numbers on. Another little one, a slightly different shape with a stick on the top. Some sort of funny flat typewriter.

'I need to make a call,' said Mr Sleight.

'The bathroom is that way.'

'On my phone.'

'The phone is just through there.'

'No, no, on this,' he held up one of the boxes.

'Oh, of course,' said Elfina. 'Of course, your moobile.'

'Mobile,' said Mr Sleight.

He pressed some buttons and held it to his ear.

Obviously madness. No wires or anything.

As Otto expected, he couldn't get it to work.

'It's the mountains,' said Elfina quickly. 'We'll have proper facilities installed later. Come downstairs and we'll go round the City together. Come along Otto, go to the bathroom. I'm looking after little Otto for the day, Mr Sleight, he's the son of an old friend.'

Shortly afterwards, Mr Sleight, only partially revived by the coffee, and little Otto, seething, were escorted down in the lift.

They sat in the big steam car. Mr Six was driving and Mr Eight sat next to Otto.

'Mr Sleight owns casinos and amusement parks on the Outside,' said Elfina to Otto, 'all over the world. I went to look for a business partner and I found him. He is going to organize coach tours for people to come in through the Gates. They'll stay in the new hotels we're building. They can see the magico shows and tour the City.'

'*Money comes, money goes,*' said Otto.

'Mr Sleight is a ruthless business man. As ruthless as I am,' said Elfina. 'Otto is exceptionally small, Mr Sleight. He may never grow any bigger.'

Mr Sleight didn't look very ruthless at the moment. He was leaning out of his seat with his mouth open.

'This is incredible! It's snowing over there! And over there, look, there's tropical parrots and stuff, how do you do that? Heck, look at the size of that bird! That's big! And it's carrying a tyre! Do they always fall over like that when they land?'

'Quite often,' said Elfina. 'That's the symbol of our City, the crate bird.'

'I haven't seen water go uphill like that before. Now this pavement is see-through, is that an aquarium down there? That building is revolving, I like that. We could shift that and rebuild it somewhere. You people are sort of humorous, aren't you? I can think of six millionaires straight off who'd come in with me and buy this whole street. We'd have to put in some burger bars. All these trees can stay though, they're pretty.'

'I'm glad you like it.'

'Like it! It's outstanding. Do sheep just sort of walk round on their own here? Those ones have gold chains round their necks. Do they go in shops? That's an environmental health issue, isn't it?'

Unknown to Mr Sleight he was looking at some members of the four-horned Hebridean Sheep clan, one of the most powerful of the sheep families and not to be trifled with under any circumstances.

'Of course, some things would have to be changed,' he continued, full of excitement. 'I gather there's no schools

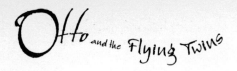

here, that's not really on. Wow! Look at the size of that snail. Now, where I come from the snails are tiny. Someone's riding that one! Look there! Now we call that abseiling. But not usually with all that shopping like that. What incredible carvings! And the clothes, all different clothes! Your people will have to get used to being photographed . . .'

And so on.

Otto, meanwhile, also saw something out of the window that he didn't expect. It was Grandpa Culpepper, wearing what had to be a false beard, walking along with someone else, also bearded. The second person, Otto was sure, was Albert.

AT THE PRISON

Otto was right. Equipped with a forged letter written using magical techniques by the widges, Grandpa Culpepper and Albert were on their way to the prison. They had taken several trams and had found the whole journey a great ordeal, especially when they went past the posters with Albert's picture on them which were tacked on to every third tree from one end of the Boulevard to the other.

Nevertheless they arrived.

The gates of the prison were predictably large and unpleasant. A guard opened a small door at the side.

Grandpa Culpepper cleared his throat and pulled his Town Hall Identity Card out of his frock coat. The picture had been taken some years before, when he still worked there. He had

had a beard then, although not quite as massive and itchy as the one he had now.

'Chief Accountant,' muttered the guard, looking at them both out of the corner of his eye.

'I am Isidor Culpepper, Chief Accountant to the Mayor and I have here a Letter of Authorization from the Minister for Modernization, Elfina Crink, requesting that you hand over convict Number G3YWJG2AXY to our custody without delay. She is needed to verify some documents.'

'And who may this be?' asked the guard.

'This is our graphology expert, Professor Copperplate. The Minister for Modernization believes that convict Number G3YWJG2AXY may be able to tell her whether certain papers at the Town Hall are, in fact, forgeries. This convict was a forger herself if my understanding is correct.'

Grandpa Culpepper produced a letter. It was covered in crests and shields and crate birds. The signature took up half the page.

'I've not come across this sort of request before,' said the guard. 'I'd better get my boss. He's had letters from the Town Hall, he can check this over.'

Albert gritted his teeth. Then, with the delicacy of a magician Grandpa Culpepper revealed a bundle of banknotes in his other hand.

At the Prison

'I am authorized to offer you these to cover any costs incurred,' he said, in a low and conspiratorial tone. 'Between you and me I suspect that our Minister may wish to release this particular convict for reasons of sentiment, possibly a distant relative, they have the same name you see, just a hunch.'

The guard reached out for the money.

'We will be happy to reimburse you when the convict is HERE,' said Grandpa Culpepper smoothly, his palm now mysteriously empty.

The guard went, shutting the door behind him.

'Don't worry,' said Grandpa Culpepper, 'he's taking the money.'

In matters of human nature Isidor Culpepper was very rarely wrong. After fifteen long minutes the door opened once more and there was the guard accompanied by a tall grey-haired woman in the black prison uniform.

While Grandpa Culpepper signed some papers for the guard and made him richer, Albert took the woman's hand and led her away from the shadow of the prison gates.

Her face was scoured with deep lines. She blinked in the sunshine and he saw that her eyes were wide and slanting and gold shot through with green and black. He had only seen one other person with such extraordinary eyes. She raised her hand to shade them. And there it was, just below her knuckles,

the faded butterfly mark that seemed almost to have worn away.

Grandpa Culpepper joined them.

'So who the skink are you two jokers?' she asked, spitting chewed bloodberry leaves on the ground.

'Honourable greetings,' said Albert. 'We know who you are. I am Albert Hush and this is my father-in-law, Isidor Culpepper. Your people need you.'

'MY people! I haven't got any people.'

'We know you are Araminta, Karmidee Queen, the architect of the Gates that saved us from annihilation, one of the greatest Karmidee who has ever lived.'

She spat again, 'I've been a lot of things since then, darling. I've had a few different names as well. Where are we going?'

Grandpa Culpepper had taken her arm and was steering her down the hill.

Albert tried to explain. 'Someone is planning to undo the magic on the Gates,' he said. 'They may be looking for you at this very moment, they may try to force you to help them, the whole City is in danger.'

'I've been a shopkeeper, a waitress, a snake charmer, an inn-keeper, a falconer . . . there's been plenty with the mark since me.'

'Do you know anything about what has been happening to the Karmidee?'

'We don't get newspapers in there, sweetheart. We don't get much.'

They were coming towards the Boulevard.

Suddenly a large piece of rusted metal, possibly once part of a tram, crashed on to the pavement in front of them. Two crate birds circled sheepishly down, picked it up between them and tried to take off again, flailing and squawking. Nest repair was an all-year-round activity.

Araminta had fallen over. She started laughing. As they picked her up and helped her along the street she went on laughing. Tears poured down her face.

Albert, sweating in his disguise, tried to speak. But Grandpa Culpepper waved at him to stop. 'Later,' he mouthed.

And so they made their way through the heart of the City and the crowds of shoppers, with Araminta pointing at things and laughing. It was mad laughter and it made Albert want to scream.

Only when they reached the PlayHouse and were climbing through the rubbish in the alleyway to get to the stage door, only then did she stop.

'I've got to find my little girl,' she said suddenly. 'Her father tricked me, he couldn't bear it when he found out. How could anyone bear it? When he saw that I would stay young, even when he was an old man. When he realized that I would always be free, only half-human, he was full of hate.

He thought I had magic powers, he thought I should make him rich. Then he had me thrown in there. They took my familiar. That's how I got old. All that matters is my little girl. I kept going for her, do you understand?'

They were in the theatre now and the others had come hurrying to meet her.

She looked round at them all, from face to face to face and the sight of Mab, small and pale-haired, made her sob afresh. 'He took my little girl, my treasure, love is love, you understand? Find her. I've got something for her, something she needs, they searched me but I hid it in my mouth. She doesn't know who she is. Find her. That's all there is.'

'I think we can help you,' said Albert.

THE Concert

The City hummed and buzzed its way through the day. Many citizens who had been looking forward to the usual midsummer festival and parade saw the poster for the concert and thought it would be fun to go out for the evening in HighNoon. After all, there was nothing else to do.

In the huts by the arena the Karmidee heard the latest rumour. There was to be a special concert, some said it had something to do with the King. Others laughed.

Amos and Lydia flew out to the hiding places in the mountains where the rest of the Karmidee had fled. Dancers were recruited. Anyone who dared to make the journey was invited to come.

Albert's father, Cornelius, had long ago denied that the King was his son. But his wife persuaded him. Together, as twilight came, they entered the city through SteepSide and made their way to the PlayHouse. Miss Fringe was with them.

Now it was dark. Citizens came from the Boulevard and streamed in through the newly-polished doors. Karmidee crept in round the side through the fire exit where Madame Morgan showed them to the gallery.

The Minister for Modernization, the Mayor, a strange looking man, a small boy and Mr Six and Mr Eight were escorted to a special box by Madame Honeybun.

When Otto saw her he almost yelled out her name. She put her fingers to her curvy lips.

'Do let us know if there is anything you need,' she said to the Mayor. 'We hope you enjoy our little entertainment.'

'Thank you,' said Mayor Crumb.

'Is there someone here called Albert Hush?' asked Elfina, 'I've got something for him.'

'I'm afraid I'm just an usherette,' said Madame Honeybun humbly.

Otto could only sit down, still a prisoner.

He heard a gasp beside him. Elfina was looking at the curtains.

'Are you all right, my dear?' asked the Mayor.

The Concert

'Oh, shut up,' said Elfina. And then, to Mr Sleight, 'This place is a dump. I'm sorry I brought you. Our Metropolitan Theatre, on the Boulevard, is wonderful.'

The expectant murmur of the audience grew quieter. The jazz band finished tuning up.

Mr Six and Mr Eight, who had not been asked to sit down by the Mayor, breathed loudly behind Otto.

The curtains opened and the two halves of the embroidered tree folded into the wings.

'Have you got this place properly surrounded?' hissed Elfina.

Mr Six sneezed, 'Yes, Minister.'

'Did you multiply again as I told you to do?'

'We did. That's why we're getting colds. We shouldn't go so high day after day. We're getting weak. We need a day off.'

'Nonsense, 2,304, that's not many. As soon as this is over I want everyone arrested. The dancers or whatever, the musicians, that usherette woman. All of them.'

In anguish Otto saw Dolores standing alone on the stage. She was wearing amazing clothes, all purple and silver and gold.

'Mayor Crumb, Minister, ladies and gentlemen,' she said, 'we will start the evening's performance with some dances written specially for the occasion.'

'What occasion?' muttered Elfina.

'Our first dance is entitled "Money buys Nothing". Thank you.'

Dolores bowed ceremoniously, the lights went out and came on again to reveal a number of dancers all holding giant gold coins. The conductor raised his long thin arms and the music began. It was eerie and strange. On the stage the dancers began to spin round and round.

The door at the back of the box creaked open and Otto turned to see Nathaniel Crane. Not just Nathaniel Crane. It was Nathaniel Crane holding Zeborah. She was asleep.

Otto jumped halfway out of his seat, only to be jammed firmly back into it by Mr Six.

Nathaniel didn't speak. He looked ill and shaky and his teeth were chattering. He just stood there, holding Zebbie and staring at Elfina.

'How do I know the child can fly?' she whispered.

Otto gave a sharp cry of horror. Nathaniel noticed him for the first time and his face contorted with misery and shame.

'She got you then,' he said. 'I saw it, in some dark place . . .'

'How do I know the child can fly?' repeated Elfina, while Mr Sleight and the Mayor looked on.

At that moment there was a crescendo of sound from the band. The dancers had made the coins into a pile and were all scrabbling to climb up. Zebbie stirred and began to wriggle.

Otto reached out and Mr Six caught his arm and twisted it behind his back. 'I don't like you,' he said chattily.

'Is this treatment necessary, my dear?' Mayor Crumb said quietly to Elfina, looking at Otto.

Elfina ignored him.

Zebbie wriggled a bit more.

Nathaniel let go of her, hoping perhaps that she would float up a little way in her sleep and he could easily take hold of her again.

She did float up, as Otto had seen her do so many times before in the safety of her loving home. She floated up and knocked very gently against the ceiling of the box.

'Give me my familiar,' said Nathaniel to Elfina.

Mr Sleight's eyes were standing out like ping-pong balls.

'Give it to me!' hissed Nathaniel.

'Zebbie!' called Otto and Mr Six clamped his sweaty hand over his mouth.

Elfina pulled something out of her pocket and Otto glimpsed a carving, a cat, like the one he wore hidden round his neck at that very moment, but smaller and without jewels.

Nathaniel snatched it from her. He seemed to be starving. He put it to his lips. At once he started to blur. The Mayor and Mr Sleight both gasped in terror.

There was a dramatic clash of cymbals from the orchestra. One dancer had made it to the top of the pile of money only to teeter there for a moment alone and then fall off dramatically on to the floor.

The lights went out for a moment.

When they came on, Nathaniel had gone and Zebbie, awake now, had drifted out from the box.

Elfina lunged at her. She was just out of reach. Unseen from below she climbed up through the dim dusty air under the dome of the roof.

'You know that kid, don't you? You called out a name. Call it again. Call it NOW!' Elfina spat at Otto.

Mr Six helpfully took his hand away from Otto's mouth.

Otto said nothing.

'I want that brat down here now with me this minute,' said Elfina. 'Do you want me to kill your father when I get my hands on him?'

'Hildegard, come here,' sang Otto, his voice husky with fear. Zebbie spiralled still further away.

'Hildegard,' called Otto, not too loudly.

'Never mind,' snapped Elfina, as one or two people looked up at them. 'What goes up must come down. One of the Normies will catch her when this charade is over.'

Dolores was on the stage again to announce the next dance. It was called 'The Frozen Army'.

The Concert

Darkness and another roll of drums. Otto had lost sight of Zebbie. Then the stage lit up and he saw her at the very top of the dome. Some of the Karmidee had seen her now. They were whispering and pointing her out to each other.

Two dancers came on the stage. One had a giant number 6 sewn onto his back and the other, an 8. They began to walk around with awkward rigid steps and there was a whisper of laughter from the gallery.

'Does this have a special meaning?' asked Mr Sleight. 'I think, by the way, I should go home and reconsider the details of the deal. Now.'

No one answered him.

Otto saw Madame Morgan walking down the aisle below, carrying Pinfracca. Granny Culpepper and Honeybun Nicely, still in her usherette uniform, came into the auditorium through a fire door opposite. Shinnabac was sitting on Granny Culpepper's shoulder. They seemed to be spacing themselves out according to a plan.

The band zipped and zapped as the first two dancers joined hands and jumped in the air and then many more came on to the stage. They stomped around.

'Forty-eight!' shouted a voice from the gallery. The dancers seemed to be pulling faces to look as stupid as possible.

'Why have those blokes got numbers on them?' asked Mr Six behind Otto.

Otto and the Flying Twins

Elfina cracked a knuckle. 'Be quiet, you idiot.'

'But, my dear,' said Mayor Crumb gently, 'I was just about to ask the same question.'

Otto could see Morgan and Pinfracca lining themselves up. He felt his heart begin to pound. They were going to do something, all the widges together.

The music was now extremely loud and the conductor seemed to be craning over his shoulder to look at the widges. 'Boom, crash BOOM!' from the drums.

The theatre seemed to be getting warmer and warmer. The air seemed to be coming alive. A blast like hot breath gathered over the citizens and rushed through the Karmidee in the gallery.

'What's happening?' cried Elfina.

But even as she spoke it was over and her voice echoed. On the stage the dancers were all still as statues. The band began a wailing lament. Still the dancers didn't move.

Now a child ran out of the wings, her long hair streaming. Otto bit his lip. It was Mab wearing a beautiful black dress. She danced and weaved between the motionless figures and then she mimed all the rudest gestures in the City, one after the other.

Wild cheers from the gallery. Even some of the citizens were clapping.

The curtains closed.

The Concert

'Stop this,' said Elfina to Mr Six and Mr Eight. 'All of you covering the doors, come in and arrest them NOW.'

Mr Six and Mr Eight didn't reply.

The Mayor and Elfina looked round at them.

'That is an order,' said the Mayor.

Nothing.

Otto dared to look over his shoulder. Then, feeling more and more excited, he reached out and prodded Mr Six in the chest.

Mr Six swayed slightly and continued to look straight ahead.

'What the——?' exclaimed Elfina.

'Zebbie!' called Otto.

But she was too confused. She kicked along the carved ceiling and began to call plaintively in her clear child's voice, 'Mummy! Mummy! Heppie! Heppie!'

'And now, may I ask you all to remain in your seats,' said Dolores, glancing anxiously up at the roof. 'Before we continue with our little show there is someone who would like a few words with you.'

The conductor was climbing up onto the stage, a thin man in a worn suit. He turned to face the audience with a weary heart. He had hoped somehow to make the farsight come true, the other possible future, full of riddles, in which Elfina did not win. He no longer hoped for that. All he could do now was warn them all . . .

'My name is Albert, King of the Karmidee,' he said. And at his name an uneasy quiet fell on citizen and Karmidee alike.

Otto waved his arms at Zebbie.

Elfina, who had been shaking Mr Eight, reached out and stopped him. He bit her hand. In a flash she raised her arm, only to be caught and held still by Mayor Crumb.

'Calm, my dear,' he murmured, 'you are not yourself.'

'The Minister for Modernization has lied to us about the roads and the mines. It is not the magicos who have caused all the problems.' Albert held his hand out to the wings and Megrafix came on to the stage, his eyes shut against the footlights.

'This is Megrafix, one of those who we Karmidee are proud to call ancestors out of respect for the fact that they lived here even before we did and carved out the tunnels and caves in the mountains and much more besides. He and some of his brothers were seized and forced to dig out those holes in the roads and make those rockfalls in the mines.'

Few of the Karmidee and none of the citizens had ever seen a caver before. Megrafix towered over Albert, dignified and frightening. He was holding a piece of rock the size of a piano above his head in one clawed hand.

'How do we know it's true?' shouted someone who looked like a miner.

Megrafix threw the rock down and it went right through the stage.

'That rock came from under your Boulevard,' said Megrafix. 'My brothers are outside this theatre now with many more.'

Perhaps some of the audience still doubted him but they kept their doubts to themselves.

'I'd like to introduce you to the woman who knows more about this City, our City, than anyone,' said Albert. 'This is Araminta.'

There was a gasp of amazement from the gallery.

Araminta stepped out of the wings.

'I am Araminta, once Queen of the Karmidee,' she said. Her voice was dusty and dry. 'I've heard some of what has been happening. I've heard that the magicos are being forced into performing in magic shows, being driven from their homes. I've heard that Outsiders will soon be coming here who will take your City away from you. Even you, the citizens, who think you know everything. You know nothing. Your City is full of magic.'

The Mayor looked round at Elfina.

'I don't care if you believe me or not, that is my warning,' continued Araminta. 'And now I'm looking for someone, my child, born on a barge in Red Moon nearly thirty years ago. I was locked in the prison and couldn't come home.'

Elfina stood up in her seat and leant over the edge of the box. She closed her fingers on the thick velvet plush on the rail and it tore like tissue paper.

'My child is a grown woman now,' said Araminta. 'She's somewhere in this City. Perhaps she's in this theatre. I'm asking her to come to me. I've longed for her every day and every night. She is a dammerung, like me.'

Her voice shook.

Albert tried to take her arm to support her but she walked to the edge of the stage.

'She doesn't know it. I was taken away from her when she was only six. I have something for her, something she needs, her familiar. They took mine from me in the prison but I hid this and it is hers. This is the secret of the dammerung, the place where her other energy is stored. The mother always carves it for her child.'

She gazed out at the audience and raised her hand. Something black on a silver chain caught the spotlights.

'AR-A-MIN-TA!' shouted some of the Karmidee, stamping their feet.

Then Otto saw his mother among the curtains in the wings, carrying a grey cat. Grandpa Culpepper appeared beside her, holding Hepzie, who was wriggling and pointing at the ceiling.

'Don't let your City be destroyed for money, as my life has

been destroyed!' cried Araminta. 'You have lived divided, but what if the enemy we despise is truly in our hearts?'

Zebbie was calling high above.

Otto pulled the chain from around his neck so quickly that he cut his skin. He knew now that the black carved cat with the ruby eyes must be Araminta's familiar. He stood up, swung it and threw it on to the stage in front of her.

She screamed and fell on it.

The audience screamed too as she began to change and to blur. She was disappearing, re-forming, a figure seen through a waterfall.

And then she was a tiger.

'Don't you see?' cried Otto to Elfina. 'Don't you know?'

Elfina, fighting off the Mayor and Mr Sleight, stepped onto the edge of the box. She stayed there a moment and then she leapt into the void above the citizens.

Horrified cries engulfed her. But she landed in the aisle safely, as a cat lands. Then she ran towards the stage and the tiger.

Otto saw his mother put the grey cat on the floor. His grandfather seemed to be trying to stop her. In the flurry Hepzie broke free. She kicked towards the roof, calling for Zeborah.

Elfina pulled herself up on to the stage and stood in front of the tiger. Her face was all twisted with pain. They stepped

towards one other. Then there was a crack like lightning and Elfina was covered in green flames.

People all over the theatre were standing up in their seats.

Dolores and her cat trembled with energy.

'YOU TOOK MY SON!' she cried.

The flames danced and died.

The screams turned to a horrified silence. Elfina was turned to stone.

Araminta the tiger threw back her head and roared. She raised her great fiery paw and something fell from between her claws. The second carving, the familiar that she had saved for her child. She pushed it along the stage until it touched the foot of the stone Elfina.

The stone cracked from top to bottom and fell open.

Nobody breathed.

There inside was another tiger. A snow tiger, silver and black.

Slowly she stepped out of the rubble and looked around her, blinking and uncertain.

The other tiger bent towards her face.

'The two joined again,' whispered Otto.

The curtains began to close.

There was an electric quiet.

'Look! Up there!' called a voice.

Up in the roof, brightly lit now, Hepzie and Zeborah had

found one another. Zebbie was no longer crying.

Hand in hand they floated in the burnished clouds of their hair. They laughed. They spun. They flickered like flames, like light itself.

They danced like butterflies.

The Snow

It was the beginning of winter in the great and mysterious City of Trees and Otto and Mab were flying over the Boulevard.

Down below Mr Six and Mr Eight were busy in the streets polishing lampposts. After he had released the magicos and the Normal Police had recovered from the freezing spell, which took some time, Mayor Crumb had given them special duties as Pavement Improvement Operatives. He had asked them only to go as high as forty-eight because otherwise he couldn't afford the wages.

The sky over the western mountains was rosy pink, evening was coming.

'Those are snow clouds,' said Mab. 'Gran said she'd make

pancakes if you want to come to our place tomorrow. NOW where are you going?'

Otto climbed steeply and circled the top of the Karmidee Tower. A long time ago, at least it seemed a long time ago, he had heard that no one knew what was on the top and it might be beetles.

'I should have known,' he said, gliding carefully back towards her.

'Should have known what?'

'Butterflies. There's two butterflies on top of the Tower.'

'Of course there are, everybody knows that.'

'Like the two butterflies on the farsight, the two that were joined again.'

'You mean your two sisters, Mr Otto, since it turned out to mean them.'

'Don't call me that.'

'But I thought you wanted to be called Otto, Otto.'

He steered higher, until the air was cold and stung his face. Far below, the arena, now a market, twinkled with flags and gilded tents. He banked round over SteepSide and slowed down to let her catch up. After all, she was carrying the tree.

'Showing off?' she asked, as soon as she was close enough.

He ignored her. The first snowflake landed on the back of his hand.

'Can we just go straight there now, Mr Otto, I'm freezing—'

They sailed on and on and at last reached the margins of the City and the wasteland where the river lay grey and quiet between its curving banks.

'Look, there they are—'

Two figures were making their way along the river path.

'Don't fall off, Otto, not with people watching.'

Otto didn't fall off. He landed a little ahead of Albert and Araminta while Mab, always more skilful with the mat, skimmed over the top of his hat and came down in just the right place and he had to jog up to where they were all saying hello.

'We think it was somewhere here,' said Albert, 'but everything looks so different, and it was at night and of course the tree's gone and it was a long time ago.'

'You think that was a long time ago,' said Araminta dryly. 'It doesn't have to be in exactly the same place, you know, so long as we have a tree.'

Mab held up the oak sapling and Araminta touched the slender trunk with reverence.

'So young,' she whispered, 'and so wise.'

'Ah, good,' said Albert. 'Here comes Megrafix.'

The caver came along the path with rapid, shambling strides. He was covered in layers of black knitted clothes coated in some sort of wax.

'I was delayed back at the mines,' he said, his eyes almost closed. 'We've almost finished the restorations, they should be opening again next week. Honourable greetings to the King.'

'And to you,' replied Albert formally, 'and thank you for coming out of the mountains at this time of year. We know it can't be pleasant.'

'It is not,' said Megrafix, 'it is extremely unpleasant, nevertheless it also an honour to assist. Something white and terribly cold landed on my nose back there. Some sort of freezing moth.'

'That's snow,' said Albert. 'Like rain but colder.'

'Unspeakable,' said Megrafix.

'This is a good place,' called Araminta, 'not too near the water.' She had climbed up a slope and the others laboured after her.

Then Megrafix bent to the ground and began to claw at it with his great hands, and frozen and hard as it was, it yielded easily and flew up behind him scattering stones and rocks and soil.

The others watched in awe. Even Araminta who had seen and done everything several times.

He worked steadily and relentlessly as if it cost him no effort and soon he had dug a hole sufficiently deep that he had to climb into it to continue.

'That's enough,' called Albert.

'A bit more,' said Araminta, 'just to be sure.'

When he had dug a bit more Megrafix climbed out. He wasn't even out of breath.

Araminta had brought a box and Albert the roll of paper, his copy of the farsight. They were going to give it back for safekeeping. She sealed the box and everyone stood back as Megrafix covered it with soil. Then they planted the tree on top.

'Do you think the roots will reach it soon?' asked Araminta.

'I'm sure they will,' said Albert.

Megrafix stamped the earth down around the tree.

'Be careful,' said Araminta.

Everyone stood quietly for a minute, while the sky and the wasteland around them grew even more cold and still.

Then Megrafix said goodbye and hurried away and Mab and Araminta decided to walk towards the mud towns together.

'I'll come part of the way with you, then I'm meeting someone,' said Araminta as they set off. 'Did you know that TigerHouse was named after me?'

Otto didn't manage to hear Mab's reply and so didn't find out if this was finally something that she didn't already know everything about.

He and Albert were going home to Hershell Buildings.

The Snow

They didn't speak for a while, just walking side by side.

'You know in the farsight it had a picture of a heart in two and then joined back into one again?' said Otto.

'Yes?'

'So whose heart do you think that was?'

'So much happened,' said Albert, after a moment, 'Araminta, Elfina, I don't know, maybe you could say it was the City itself.'

More snowflakes were falling now.

'You know it's your mother's birthday on Monday,' he added. 'You haven't forgotten?'

'I'm getting her a scarf,' said Otto. 'Madame Morgan's finding it for me. Did you know that the widges have their own shop? That's where they get all their amazing clothes.'

'I'm giving her this,' said Albert. And he took from his pocket the giant moonstone that Megrafix had entrusted to Otto in the Billiard Room.

They both stopped to look at it.

'Like moonlight,' said Otto, 'like a piece of light.'

'Think she'll like it?'

Otto looked up at his father's quiet face.

'She told me the other day that I should be proud of you, because you did something for the Karmidee. You saved them just like Araminta did.'

'Your MOTHER said that!?'

'Yes, Dad, she did.'

Albert gazed at the looming City, lit now with thousands of street lamps, half lost in a mist of falling snow.

'Your mother said that . . .' he whispered.

'Look, look, over there!' Otto was pointing back the way they had come. A tiger, rust and black in the dim light, crossed the path. Then something like a shadow followed it, something that seemed a part of the frozen ground and the snow. The shadow crossed the path again, nearer now, and then it came towards them and its shape became clearer and they saw a white cloud of breath.

The snow tiger held them with her golden eyes. She walked right up to them. Suddenly she was so close that she had only to lower her magnificent head and she was touching Albert's hand.

Otto felt the heat of her body as she passed him. Then she was gone again, away into the twilight.